Marcus was ner...

He didn't like that feeling.

What was it about Joanna that so strongly affected him?

Just looking at her—the way her hair had gotten blown by the wind and was even messier than usual, the way her dark eyes met his for one naked moment before moving on, and the way it seemed to take an effort for her to smile as naturally as she had Friday night before he'd kissed her—all reminded him more forcefully than words or any lectures he might have given himself that he might already have crossed into territory he'd never been in before.

That maybe it was too late to go back.

* * *

The Hunt for Cinderella: Seeking Prince Charming

Dear Reader,

Writing a new book is always an adventure. So is life. Both are like going on a long road trip; you never really know what's coming. You might plan your route, what you'll see and do, but invariably something happens to thwart your plans, and you have to adapt and change accordingly.

This first book of the third Hunt for Cinderella series was planned more than three years ago, with the expectation that it would be published in late 2011. But in July 2010, just after I'd first begun writing it, my husband was diagnosed with a terminal illness, and everything else I was doing had to be put aside so that I could spend all my time with him.

My husband passed away in January of 2012 and it took almost a year for me to feel as if I could write again. I'm so glad that *Holiday by Design* and the two books that will follow in the series are finally going to be in readers' hands. It was fun for me to write about Joanna and Marcus and to revisit characters from the previous Hunt for Cinderella books. I hope you enjoy the story and would love to hear from you. You can find me at www.patriciakay.com.

With warmest wishes to all,

Patricia Kay

Holiday by Design

—

Patricia Kay

HARLEQUIN® SPECIAL EDITION®

Recycling programs
for this product may
not exist in your area.

ISBN-13: 978-0-373-65778-0

HOLIDAY BY DESIGN

Copyright © 2013 by Patricia A. Kay

Printed in U.S.A.

www.Harlequin.com

PATRICIA KAY

Formerly writing as Trisha Alexander, Patricia Kay is a *USA TODAY* bestselling author of more than forty-eight novels of contemporary romance and women's fiction. She lives in Houston, Texas. To learn more about her, visit her website at www.patriciakay.com.

This book is dedicated to my first writing teacher, the wonderful Bunny Paine-Clemes, who's always known how to inspire and draw the best from her students, and to my longtime "PAL" from West Houston RWA, Pat O'Dea Rosen, who has become a dear friend, an always-helpful critique partner and a second Mama to my cats.

Chapter One

"Happy birthday, dear Joanna...happy birthday to youuu."

As the Spinelli family raised their glasses in a birthday toast, Joanna smiled at the gathered clan and hoped it didn't show that her heart wasn't in it.

Thirty years old.

Today she was thirty years old, and on this milestone birthday, instead of being well on her way to a successful career in fashion design, married to the man of her dreams and—at the very least—pregnant with her first child, she was still struggling for recognition in her chosen field, still employed as a part-time assistant to her former lover—who had dumped her less than two weeks ago!—and she was so far from being pregnant with any child she might as well forget about ever becoming a mom.

My life needs a major overhaul. Oh, who am I kidding? My life needs a miracle.

And tonight, adding insult to insult, she didn't even have a date. But her state of woe wasn't her family's fault, was it? So she had been doing her best to look cheerful and happy to be here with them tonight. And heaven knew, they'd tried to make her feel good. Her mom had knitted Joanna a gorgeous, dark red, oversize cashmere shawl—perfect for chilly Seattle fall weather—and her dad, always generous toward his one and only daughter, had given her a hundred-dollar gift card, while her four brothers had pitched in to buy her an iPad, which was incredibly sweet of them.

In fact, she still couldn't believe they'd done it. She could hardly wait to buy some design software she'd been eyeing. Now she'd be able to work no matter where she was without having to lug her heavier laptop.

And then there was Granny Carmela, her dad's mom, who had tucked a check for five hundred dollars into her card. Bless Granny, Joanna thought as she gave her eighty-six-year-old grandmother an extra hug. Such a loving, generous gift. If only five hundred dollars would solve Joanna's financial problems…but that was another story, one Joanna didn't want to even think about today. She subscribed to Scarlett O'Hara's philosophy that anything bad could be thought about tomorrow.

Her family was a good bunch, for all that she complained about her dad's controlling ways and her mom's seeming subservience and the way her brothers sometimes acted like neanderthals. But what were families for, if not to bear the brunt of complaints? Who better to blame when your life went offtrack?

"Who wants a slice of cake?" her mother asked with an eager smile.

"Make mine a wedge," said Tony, Joanna's oldest brother.

"Tony," his wife, Sharon, warned, looking meaningfully at his waistline.

"I know, I know." He grinned. "German chocolate's my favorite, Share."

"Everything's your favorite," she grumbled.

"I'll be good tomorrow. I promise."

They all laughed. Tony's promises concerning food were rarely serious. Or adhered to.

After cake and their favorite MORA ice cream had been consumed, Joanna figured she'd stayed the obligatory amount of time and could now leave without hurting her mother's feelings.

"Oh, honey, I thought you were going to spend the night," her mother protested, dark eyes filled with disappointment.

Joanna's parents lived in the same small house in Georgetown that they'd lived in since the day they bought it. Located south of Seattle, their area was the oldest residential neighborhood in the city and had been a great place to grow up in. "Can't, Mom. I need to get an early start tomorrow."

"But, honey…tomorrow's Thursday. You're off on Thursdays."

Joanna had an arrangement with her former lover/ boss. She only worked four days a week. She would have preferred having her three days off in a row, but beggars couldn't be choosers, and her job not only paid well but gave her full benefits. "Yes, but…"

"Ann Marie, give the girl a break," Joanna's father said.

"But, Tony, she is off, and I thought we could—"

"I meant I have to work on my collection," Joanna said, interrupting her mother. She desperately needed to have at least twelve designs ready to show, and possibly more—if she could find a place to show them, of course—and right now she only had nine completed and had only just begun to work on the tenth.

Of course, if she didn't manage to raise more money—that five-hundred-dollar birthday gift would barely pay a third of what she already owed on her Visa card—she was gonna be dead in the water.

Pushing her dismal thoughts out of her mind, Joanna managed to keep a smile on her face as she said her goodbyes and gathered up her gifts. The drive to her small apartment in Tremont, a convenient area she loved for its eclectic atmosphere, only took about twenty minutes.

Still, it was midnight before she fell into bed—actually, her sofa—and when the alarm went off at six, she groaned, sorely tempted to shut it off and go back to sleep for another hour or two. Tabitha, her ten-year-old gray cat, obviously felt the same way, for she burrowed under Joanna's abandoned pillow and shut her eyes again.

Still half-asleep, Joanna stumbled her way into her minuscule kitchenette and turned on the coffeemaker. After filling Tabitha's food bowl and putting out fresh water for her, Joanna headed for the shower. An hour later, dressed in jeans and a warm sweater—as usual, mid-September in the Pacific Northwest was a true harbinger of winter—thick socks and her favorite clogs, she headed to her converted living room and her worktable where she had a gorgeous piece of sea-green velvet.

Joanna sipped at her coffee and smiled. Despite the early rising time, it was great to have a whole day to work on her designs. So what if she was thirty years old and hadn't yet met her goals? Thirty wasn't the end of the world. Depending on how you thought of it, thirty was actually a beginning. So what if she was going to run out of money soon? She'd manage. She always did. And she'd never had to ask her parents for money, although Lord knows, she'd thought about it. But they didn't have a lot, and they were getting older. Each time she'd been tempted to approach them, she'd stopped herself. They'd done enough for her in helping her pay her college and art school costs.

Soon she was so engrossed in the creation of her new design, the hours flew by. It was only when her stomach rumbled in hunger that she finally stopped working. Glancing at the clock, she was shocked to realize it was almost three. Her fridge yielded tuna salad that still smelled okay, so she fixed a sandwich and cut up an apple to go with it, then headed back to the dress form, where the velvet wasn't draping quite the way she'd hoped.

Maybe the velvet had been a mistake. For this collection, she'd chosen to work with lighter, more forgiving fabrics—chiffons, silks, laces and the like. But the velvet had virtually cried out to be made into a one-shoulder, floor-length evening dress. The moment she'd seen it, she'd pictured it worn by Prince William's beautiful wife. In fact, Joanna had a large photo of the duchess tacked onto her enormous bulletin board—a constant reminder of the effect she hoped to achieve and the kind of woman she hoped to attract as a client.

She was halfway through her late lunch when her cell rang. The ring tone announced the call was from Georgie Prince, her BFF.

"Hey, girl," Georgie said.

"Hey." Knowing a call from Georgie always stretched to at least half an hour, Joanna sank onto a kitchen chair and put her feet up on its neighbor.

"What're you up to today?" Georgie asked.

"Working on that new design."

"The one you emailed me?"

"Yep."

"Oh, Joanna, it's gorgeous. You know, I wish you'd make that dress for me. It'd be perfect for the holidays. Zach and I have several parties, and I'd love to have that dress for at least one of them."

Joanna sat up. "Really? You're serious?"

"Never more. I absolutely love it."

"I'd love to make it for you. How soon would you need it?"

"Middle of November. Is that doable?"

"I'll make it doable."

"So, how'd the party go last night?"

Joanna sighed. "It was nice."

"You don't sound sure."

"No, it really was. The boys gave me an iPad. And my mom knitted me the most beautiful cashmere shawl." Joanna's mother had recently bought out her longtime employer, and now was the proud owner of a small yarn shop.

"Red?"

Joanna laughed. "Yes, red."

"Your mother never stops trying, does she?"

Georgie was referring to the fact that Joanna preferred to wear black. Even today her jeans were black, as was her sweater.

"She keeps thinking she'll change me," Joanna said.

"Just like my mom," Georgie said.

Joanna refrained from saying what she was thinking, that Georgie *had* changed, that Cornelia Fairchild Hunt, Georgie's mother, had been right all along, whereas she, Joanna, was never going to be other than who she was, no matter who might prefer her to be different.

"So, are you feeling any better about the big three-oh now?" Georgie asked.

"Yeah, I've decided I'm fine with being thirty." Yet even as she said it, Joanna knew her earlier pep talk to herself had begun to wear off. "I just wish I had more to look forward to," she added in a burst of honesty. This was not something she would have admitted to anyone other than Georgie.

"Oh, stop that. You have your whole life to look forward to."

"Said by a woman who's already got a fantastic career, not to mention a real, live Prince Charming." Joanna hated the tinge of envy in her voice, because she was genuinely happy for her best friend. Zach Prince was perfect for Georgie, and Joanna had loved him the moment she'd met him.

"You're going to have a fabulous career, and it'll be much more exciting than mine," Georgie said. "And as far as that perfect guy goes, it's going to happen for you, too, and probably when you least expect it. I know I certainly didn't expect it."

"Yeah, yeah, I'm sure you're right. Don't pay any attention to me. I guess I'm just tired right now. And discouraged."

"Did you go to Pacific Savings like I suggested?" Georgie asked.

"I went yesterday on my lunch hour. And I chalked up my fifteenth 'no' in as many days."

Georgie fell silent for a moment. Then she said, "Maybe I could get Harry to call Pacific Savings."

"No! Don't you dare ask him to call them." Joanna

might be temporarily discouraged, but she had pride. Harry Hunt, the billionaire Seattle legend who had recently married Georgie's mother, didn't even know her. Well, he might know who she was, and that she was Georgie's friend, but otherwise, she was a stranger to him. If Joanna wouldn't even ask her own father for help, she certainly wasn't going to go begging to Harry Hunt!

"Harry wouldn't mind," Georgie said.

"Maybe not. But I mind."

"You're so stubborn. Everyone needs a little help sometimes."

"Spoken by the woman who would have strangled anyone who tried to help her in the past."

There was silence for a moment. Then Georgie said, "What will you do?"

Joanna grimaced. "I really don't have a choice."

"You'll keep working for Chick?"

"I don't want to, but I also don't want to try to find another job, either. I mean, how many part-time jobs can there be that pay as well as mine?"

"I don't want you to keep working for Chick, either," Georgie said fiercely. "He's a total jerk."

"I realize that now. I seem to attract that kind of person. In lovers and in bosses." Joanna was grateful Georgie was a good enough friend she never rubbed Joanna's nose in the fact that she'd warned her against getting involved with both Chick and Ivan Klemenko— a designer she'd done some work for who'd stolen her ideas and passed them off as his own—from day one. And Joanna, as usual, had willfully gone her own way…and paid the price. She sighed heavily. What was done was done. And nothing was going to change the past now. "Look, that's enough about me. Let's talk about you for a change."

For the next ten minutes, Georgie filled Joanna in on the doings in the Prince household. Finally, when Joanna was about to say she'd better get back to work, Georgie said, "I have something else to tell you. But you have to promise you won't laugh."

"Laugh? Why would I laugh? What have you done now?"

"Well, after all the years I've said I didn't want children…" Georgie's voice trailed off.

It took a few seconds for the import of Georgie's statement to sink in. Then Joanna squealed. "Georgie! Are you pregnant? I don't believe it!"

Georgie laughed, the sound filled with joy. "I know. I don't believe it, either."

"Oh, Georgie, that's wonderful." Joanna told herself she was not jealous. She did not begrudge this to her friend. "How…how far along are you?" Georgie and Zach had been married in April.

"A little over three months. I went to the doctor yesterday."

"Wow."

"Yes. Wow."

"You're happy, aren't you?"

"Oh, Joanna, I'm so happy I can't believe it. We haven't told anyone yet except my mom, not even the children." Zach had three children from his previous marriage. The youngest, Emma, was just four. The oldest, Katie, was eleven. Remembering how unhappy Katie had been at first, before Georgie had won her over, Joanna said, "What do you think Katie will say?"

"I don't know. I'm a little worried, to tell you the truth."

"I'll bet she'll be fine. Most girls love having a little sister."

"Except she already has a little sister."

"I know, but think about yourself. You have three younger sisters, and you once told me you were thrilled about every one of them."

They talked another ten minutes about the baby, which was due the middle of March, and about how the velvet gown could work even around a baby bump, then began to say their goodbyes. Before hanging up, Georgie said, "Hang in there, Jo."

Joanna made a face. "I will. Actually, on Monday, I plan to visit Up and Coming, that gallery I told you about. Who knows? They might agree to let me show my collection there, and then maybe one of the banks will change its mind and lend me the money I need." She made a face. "Yeah, and I'll probably win the lottery, too."

"See? I knew you'd come up with another idea," Georgie said, completely ignoring Joanna's attempt at dark humor. "And if the gallery and loan don't work out for you, Zach and I will be happy to finance the rest of the collection."

"I know. You've already told me that. But I can't let you do that, Georgie. What if…" But Joanna couldn't give voice to her greatest fear, not even to Georgie.

"Do not say it, Joanna! You will not fail. Your collection will be a huge hit. Huge. Listen, I know fashion. So do my sisters. And we all love your clothes."

With that ringing endorsement still reverberating in her ears, Joanna said goodbye. But the moment the connection was broken, her spirits flagged again. Yes, Georgie and her sisters did love her clothes, but they were prejudiced.

So even if the owner of Up and Coming said yes to her on Monday, and even if one of the banks did change its mind and lend her the money to finish the collection, she could still fail.

As soon as the thought formed, she got mad at herself. What was wrong with her? Why was she even entertaining such a negative idea? She was not and never had been a negative person. She was a chance taker. She believed in herself and in her talent.

Georgie was right. She would succeed!

No matter what it took.

"Will you be home for dinner tonight, Marcus?"

Marcus Osborne Barlow III shook his head. "I'm afraid not, Mother. Walker and I have a dinner meeting scheduled." Walker Creighton was the family's longtime lawyer and also sat on the board of Barlow International. When his mother didn't answer, Marcus looked up from the *Seattle Times*. Her grayish-blue eyes—whose color he'd inherited—seemed stricken. "What's wrong?"

She looked down at her half-eaten English muffin. "It's nothing. Don't worry."

It was never nothing with his mother. Ever since his father's unexpected death of a heart attack fifteen years earlier just before Marcus's twenty-first birthday in his third year of college, Laurette Bertrand Barlow had been incapable of handling much more than what to have for dinner. And sometimes she seemed incapable of doing even that. She hadn't always been this way. When his father was alive, she'd been a different woman. Or had she? Maybe, like most young people, he'd simply been too wrapped up in his own life to notice.

Marcus finished the last of his coffee and put the paper down. He'd learned that coaxing his mother didn't work, so he simply sat there quietly. After long seconds, she finally met his gaze. "It's Vanessa."

"What about her?" he said more sharply than he'd intended.

"She talked back to me last night. I will not be talked to that way, Marcus."

Vanessa was Marcus's twenty-year-old sister. Only five when their father died, she idolized Marcus. And he adored her, even as he sometimes despaired of making her into the kind of young lady who would do the Barlow family and company proud. The kind of young lady a man so seldom found nowadays.

"What did she say to you?" he asked.

His mother flushed. "She told me I was stupid."

"Stupid!" Marcus was appalled. Sometimes he understood why Vanessa was impatient with their mother. After all, Laurette was often difficult to deal with. But showing disrespect, no matter the provocation, would not be tolerated. Especially since Creighton had been urging Marcus to assume more international business travel. How could he take charge abroad when his mother and sister still expected him to mediate their disagreements?

Suppressing a sigh, he said, "I'll speak to her." He put down his paper, rose and headed for the stairs.

Five minutes later, he knocked on Vanessa's bedroom door. In the mood he was in, he almost went in without waiting for an answer, but if he was to lead by example, good manners dictated he wait.

"Is that you, Mother?" was followed by the door opening. Vanessa, blond hair still tousled from sleep, stood there in a very short blue bathrobe and bare feet. Her eyes, dark blue like their father's had been, lost their defiant glare when she realized it was her brother at the door and not her mother.

"I thought you'd already gone to the office," she said, smiling.

"I have a meeting in Kirkland today." Wasn't she cold?

"Oh."

"Don't you have a class this morning?" Vanessa was taking a couple of design classes at the Art Institute of Seattle.

"It was canceled. The instructor's wife went into labor yesterday, so I thought I'd check out that new exhibit at the Frye." She tightened the skimpy robe around her. For the first time, she seemed to sense his mood. "Is something wrong, Marcus?"

"Mother says last night you called her stupid."

Vanessa shook her head. "That's not quite true."

"Not quite true? How can something be not quite true?"

"I didn't call her stupid. I said what she'd said was stupid. That's not the same thing."

"You're splitting hairs. Talking to your mother that way is disrespectful, and you know it."

"Don't you even want to know what it was she said?"

"No. It doesn't matter. What matters is that you must always treat your mother with respect."

"But, Marcus—"

"No buts."

"So I can't even disagree with her?" The defiant glare was back in full force.

"I didn't say that. It's entirely possible to have a difference of opinion without being rude...or disrespectful."

Vanessa rolled her eyes. "You know, Marcus, as much as I love you, you have a tendency to sound like some old man. I mean, come on, no one talks the way you do anymore."

"Excuse me?" he said stiffly. If he sounded older than he was, maybe it was because he'd never had a choice. Did she ever think of that? A week after his father's death, he'd had to put on a suit and tie and meet with Barstow's board to convince them he'd be capable of assuming the company's reins in five years. It wasn't something he'd ever wanted to do, but who else was there to do it?

And this was what his sister thought of him now? Suddenly he saw Vanessa through the eyes of their mother. Maybe Laurette had been right all along. Maybe he did spoil Vanessa.

"I've been defending your bad behavior long enough," he said, hardening his heart. "Mother is right. From now on, things are going to be different. You will apologize to Mother. And you will be grounded for the weekend."

"Grounded! I'm twenty years old! You can't ground me."

"I most certainly can. The fact that you are twenty years old has no bearing on anything, especially when you still sometimes behave as if you are ten. Remember this, Vanessa. You live under my roof. You are dependent on me. That means you follow my rules. If you don't want to follow my rules, then you're free to find a place of your own."

Her mouth dropped open. He knew she was shocked, for he had never before talked to her this way.

"Now get dressed and come downstairs and apologize to your mother. I'm leaving for my meeting, and when I come home tonight, I expect you to be here. And that you will have already given Mother your sincere apology."

As he turned to go back downstairs, he fully expected to hear her door slam, because Vanessa had a temper. Instead, there was silence. He strode down the hall, then stopped. Shaking his head, he turned around and walked back to his sister's door. He was sorry to have spoken so harshly. After all, he did know how difficult his mother could be and how she could strain anyone's patience.

He grasped the knob of Vanessa's door, but he didn't open it. He couldn't. At the age of twenty, he'd had to thrust aside all his dreams and hopes for the future. He'd had to grow up fast. To assume responsibility for both his siblings and his mother, not to mention an entire corporation and the workers who depended on him.

If he wanted Vanessa to be a credit to him and to their family, to become the lovely woman he knew she could be, then this rebelliousness of hers needed to be reined in.

He released the knob and headed for the stairs. This time, he didn't look back.

Chapter Two

On Monday, Chick left for Oregon and a buying trip, so Joanna put the phone on voice mail and took a couple of hours for lunch. Luckily, it was a pretty day—cool but sunny—so she walked the fifteen blocks from Chick's office to Up and Coming's trendy location in Belltown, right on the fringes of Queen Anne.

Joanna had read about Up and Coming in Phoebe Lancaster's column in the July issue of *Around Puget Sound* magazine. The gallery featured new artists, and apparently they weren't limited to painters and sculptors because sometime this fall they were scheduled to showcase the work of a jewelry designer. When Joanna had read that, she'd immediately wondered if it might be possible to have *her* work shown there, too. After all, she was an artist—every bit as much as someone who designed jewelry. The idea had excited her, and she'd filed it in the back of her mind, thinking it might be something she could explore in the future.

Well, the future was here. Up and Coming was one of her last resorts. Maybe her *very* last resort.

Located on a shady, tree-lined street where several restaurants and boutiques mingled with half a dozen galleries, Up and Coming had an elegant facade with double walnut doors flanked by old-fashioned gas lamps. Its two large display windows held vividly colored ceramic vases and bowls, along with fanciful animals carved from what looked like mahogany. One—a mouse with an impudent expression—made her smile. It also gave her hope that the owner had an open mind about what constituted art.

Tiny silver bells tinkled when Joanna opened the door and walked inside. A tall blonde with a severe hairdo, slicked back and fashioned into a tiny ballerina bun, looked up at Joanna's entrance.

"Yes?" She didn't smile. Instead, her gaze flicked to Joanna's knee-high boots with their four-inch heels, then traveled up and over her diamond-patterned black stockings, black miniskirt and tight leather jacket.

"Hello," Joanna said brightly. Walking over to the counter where the woman stood with an open catalogue in front of her, Joanna extended her right hand. "I'm Joanna Spinelli. I wrote to you last week about the possibility of showing my work here."

The blonde ignored the hand. "And what might that work be?" Still no smile. In fact, her eyes, a frosty dark blue that matched her long-sleeved, high-necked wool dress, were looking at Joanna as if she had wandered into the gallery by mistake.

"I'm a, um, fashion designer." Joanna could have kicked herself for the hesitation in her voice. "You may have heard of my label? JS Designs? I did the bridesmaids' gowns for the Fairchild wedding in the spring. There was a spread in *Puget Sound Magazine*—"

"We are an art gallery, Miss…"

"Spinelli," Joanna repeated.

The blonde fingered her double strand of pearls.

"Spinelli." This was said as if the name itself was distasteful.

"And I know you're an art gallery," Joanna said, "but I read an article recently about how you'll be showing some jewelry by a local artist and I thought—"

"Yes. Well. That designer is the sister of the owner."

"Oh." Joanna's heart sank. This was not going well. "Um, then, perhaps I could speak to the owner? I brought my portfolio with me to show—"

"Mr. Barlow is a busy man and rarely here."

Telling herself not to be cowed by this snobby woman, Joanna drew herself up to her full five feet three plus the four-inch heels. "And you are?"

The blonde's eyes narrowed as if she couldn't quite believe Joanna had the audacity to ask her name. For a moment, Joanna was sure she didn't intend to answer, but finally she said, "I am the manager of the gallery. Brenda Garfield."

"It's nice to meet you, Ms. Garfield. Now, if you could just take a look at my designs…"

Lifting the portfolio to the glass countertop, Joanna opened it to the first photograph. The model, a favorite of Joanna's, was an ethereal-looking redhead—a Nicole Kidman type, Joanna had always thought—and she was wearing one of Joanna's hand-crocheted dresses— a pale apricot confection with a swirling skirt, worn over a matching silk slip. The photographer had created the illusion of sun-kissed clouds drifting around her. It had cost Joanna the earth to have these photographs shot, but she figured the investment in her future was worth it.

The Garfield woman barely glanced at the photo.

Determined not to give up, Joanna turned the page.

This photo featured a willowy, dark-haired model standing on a moonlit balcony. She was wearing a midnight-blue satin evening dress overlaid with ecru lace and held a champagne glass in her hand.

Brenda Garfield's eyes briefly skimmed the photograph, then rose to meet Joanna's own. "I doubt Mr. Barlow would be interested," she said coldly.

Joanna would have liked to say what she was thinking, but stopped herself just in time. Never burn bridges. How often had her mother advised that? "I'll just leave my card," she said politely. "He can look at my designs on my website."

"As you wish."

Joanna figured the card would be thrown in the trash the moment she was out the door. Suppressing a sigh, she closed her portfolio and, head held high, said, "Thank you for your time."

Joanna waited until she'd walked outside and out of sight of the snooty Brenda Garfield before giving vent to her feelings. *I won't cry,* she told herself as the full weight of her crushed hopes and lost dreams bore down on her shoulders.

"I might as well forget about this damn place," she said aloud. "She isn't going to tell the owner about me." For one second, she almost pitched the album containing the photos into the trash container standing on the curb.

But something stopped her.

Maybe the portfolio was worthless. Maybe no one else would ever look at her designs again. Maybe things looked dark right now, but tomorrow was another day.

And she was not a quitter.

Besides, these photos were too beautiful and had cost too much to end up in a public trash receptacle.

Cornelia Fairchild Hunt had just finished arranging a large bouquet of fresh-cut flowers in the morning room when Martha, her longtime housekeeper who had come along with her when she'd moved into her new husband's mansion in the spring, walked into the room.

"Mrs. Hunt, Georgie's on the phone."

"Thank you, Martha." Cornelia smiled, always delighted to hear from her oldest daughter. Now that Georgie had married such a wonderful man, and was stepmother to three equally wonderful children, she always had interesting news and funny stories to recount. And soon, to Cornelia's delight, Georgie would be adding another baby to Cornelia's growing list of grandchildren. Life was good.

Cornelia lifted the phone. "Hello, Georgie."

"Hi, Mom. What're you up to today?"

"Oh, nothing much. Just doing some flower arranging. Thinking about having a toes-up later."

They chatted for a while, and then Georgie said, "Mom, I wanted to bounce something off you."

"What, dear?" Cornelia listened thoughtfully as Georgie explained about her best friend Joanna Spinelli's dilemma, finishing up with "I just wish I knew the owner of that gallery so I could put in a good word for Joanna. Unfortunately, he's older than me, and I don't believe I've ever met him. Do you by any chance know him?"

"Well, first of all, what's his name?"

"Oh, sorry. Marcus Barlow. You might have read about him. He's the head of Barlow International, that import/export company that's doing so much business in Asia. *Seattle Today* did a big feature article on him back in May. I also read somewhere that he was going to appear on *60 Minutes*."

"Actually, Georgie, I've met Mr. Barlow. He was seated next to me at the heart association fund-raiser last month. He's a really charming young man."

For a moment, there was silence. Then Georgie exclaimed, "Mom! That's wonderful. I can't believe you know him."

"Well, I don't know him well, of course, but we did have the loveliest conversation that evening. And, in fact, on the drive home, I mentioned to Harry that we ought to invite Mr. Barlow to one of our dinner parties." She remembered how, even though Marcus Barlow was an attractive, influential, wealthy man, and women had fawned over him all evening, he hadn't paid them much attention. He'd seemed happier talking to Cornelia, even though she was old enough to be his mother. There was something about him that had really touched her that evening. Afterward, she'd thought perhaps she'd sensed a quality of loneliness in him and she'd responded to it.

"Do you think you could—"

Georgie didn't have to finish her question. Cornelia knew what her daughter wanted from her. "I wouldn't mind calling him and mentioning Joanna, if that's what you're suggesting. As I said, I wanted to invite him to dinner anyway."

"Oh, gosh, that would be wonderful. But you could never let Joanna know you'd done so."

"Why? Do you think she'd be upset?"

"Oh, you know how she is."

"Well, darling, if what you've told me is accurate, if anyone needs a fairy godmother, it's Joanna."

Even though thousands of miles separated them, Cornelia knew Georgie was smiling. "And there's no one better to fulfill that role than you, mother of mine."

After they'd hung up, Cornelia decided she liked the idea of being Joanna's fairy godmother. For years Cornelia had had all she could handle just keeping body and soul together and making sure her four daughters didn't suffer from the sins of their father. She hadn't the wherewithal to play Lady Bountiful. But now—especially since Harry had, over her objections, settled some sixty million dollars on her the week after their wedding—she had the means to do whatever she wanted to do.

Now, just where had she put that business card of Marcus Barlow's?

Marcus had to pass right by the gallery on his way back to his office, and he couldn't resist stopping in. Up and Coming was an indulgence, and he knew it—it barely paid for itself—but he didn't care. He'd had to give up his dream of becoming a working artist when his father's death had redirected his life. Up and Coming was his way of staying a part of the art community.

Granted, owning a gallery was a far cry from living his art, but at least now he felt he was contributing something important. From the day he'd opened its doors, Up and Coming had featured the work of new and struggling artists. Because of the boost he'd given them, Marcus could count half a dozen in the past few years who had gone on to make a success of their chosen careers.

Smiling, thinking how much he enjoyed his role with Up and Coming, he felt all his worries and responsibilities fade away as he entered the gallery.

Brenda, as always, seemed glad to see him. When the gallery had first opened, Marcus had been concerned about stopping by as often as he wanted to. He hadn't wanted Brenda to think he questioned her abilities as his manager or that he was checking up on her. He needn't have worried. Those thoughts never seemed to enter her mind.

In fact, sometimes she seemed *too* glad to see him. As a result, he was careful to maintain a strictly professional relationship. During the few times she had attempted to discuss his or her personal life, he had always steered her back to business.

Today was no exception. "You look tired," she said.

He shrugged. "I wondered if you'd had a chance to contact Jamison Wells."

"We talked right after lunch."

"And?"

"He's thrilled, of course."

"Is November a good month for him?"

"He says yes. He guaranteed us forty paintings."

"Great. When can we see them?"

"I told him you'd call to fix a time."

After Brenda brought him up-to-date about two more new artists they were considering for future shows, she excused herself and headed toward the restroom. A moment later, the telephone rang, and Marcus walked behind the counter to answer it. After giving the caller directions to the gallery, he disconnected the call and was about to walk away when he noticed a business card on the floor next to the waste basket. He picked it up and glanced at it.

J S Designs
When you want to feel like a princess

There was a name in small type at the bottom—Joanna Spinelli—a phone number and a website address, but nothing else. The message on the card intrigued him. What kind of designs was the woman talking about? He was just about to take the card back to the office and look up the website when Brenda returned.

Seeing the card in his hand, she frowned. "I thought I threw that away."

"You missed the basket. I found this on the floor." When she said nothing further, he added, "What kind of designer is she?"

Brenda made a face. "She designs clothes. I told her I doubted we'd ever be interested in anything like that."

He nodded. Normally he would have agreed with Brenda. Fashion had never interested him, especially couture fashion. But for some reason, he was curious about this woman's designs. He guessed the statement about feeling like a princess was what had intrigued him.

Casually, he put the card in his jacket pocket. Brenda noticed, though. He saw her lips tighten. Deciding he owed her no explanation, he said he had to be going and would drop by again later in the week.

Back at his office, he pulled out the business card and looked up the woman's website. He wasn't sure what he'd expected, but it certainly wasn't what he found.

The dresses and gowns featured on the website were exactly the kinds of clothes he would like to see his sister wear, exactly the kinds of clothes he would want a wife of his to wear. They were stunning—beautiful and elegant. The Spinelli woman hadn't exaggerated. Her clothes *were* fit for a princess.

He wished there were more of them on the website instead of the half dozen featured. He also wondered about the designer herself. There was no picture, no bio. Just contact information.

He was about to do a search of the designer's name when his secretary buzzed him to say Cornelia Hunt was on the line. He smiled and picked up the phone. "Hello, Cornelia. What a nice surprise."

"Is it? I've been meaning to call you ever since the night we met. And today I had the perfect excuse. Harrison and I are having a small dinner party next month on the eighth, and I was hoping you could come."

"The eighth..." Marcus checked his calendar, saw that the evening was free and said, "That sounds good."

After she gave him the particulars, she said, "If you've got a few more minutes, there's one other thing I wanted to ask you about."

"I have as many minutes as you need."

"I know you own an art gallery in Belltown."

"Yes. Up and Coming."

"And you sometimes feature artists and designers who work with unusual materials. I believe my daughter mentioned a jewelry designer whose work will be shown in October?"

"That's right."

"Have you ever considered showing the work of a fashion designer?"

Taken aback, Marcus wondered if Cornelia Hunt was a mind reader. It was almost as if she'd known he was thinking about Joanna Spinelli. "I haven't given it a lot of thought," he said, "but yes, I have considered it."

"In that case, I wanted to recommend someone. This young woman is very talented. In fact, she designed the bridesmaids' dresses for my wedding and she also designed the bridal gown my oldest daughter wore when *she* was recently married. Her name is Joanna Spinelli, and she's currently working on finishing her first collection and I'd really like to be able to help her out a bit. So I thought if you were interested I could introduce you."

"It's odd you should mention Ms. Spinelli, because she visited the gallery today and left her card. In fact, when you called, I had just finished looking at her designs on her website."

"And what did you think of her work?"

"I was favorably impressed."

"Lovely," Cornelia Hunt said.

"In fact," he said, thinking aloud, "it's possible we could combine her designs and my sister's jewelry into one show." That would give Vanessa a boost, too, plus make for a more interesting evening for possible buyers. "I forgot to mention that the jewelry designer we're featuring this fall is my sister, Vanessa."

"That sounds wonderful."

The more Marcus thought about it, the more logical his idea seemed. Of course, everything would depend on whether Vanessa liked the Spinelli woman and her designs and vice versa and whether the clothing and jewelry would be complementary, but it was certainly worth exploring.

"So, would you like me to arrange a meeting?" Cornelia asked.

"It's not really necessary. I have Ms. Spinelli's card. I'll give her a call."

"That's even better, because the truth is, I was hoping Joanna didn't have to know that I'd talked to you about her. She's…rather proud, you see."

"I understand. I'm rather proud myself."

Cornelia laughed softly. "There's nothing wrong with a little pride. It makes one work harder, don't you think?"

"I couldn't agree more."

Joanna didn't call Georgie after the fiasco at Up and Coming. Normally she would have. But right now she was too bummed to talk to anyone, even Georgie. It was all very well to tell herself she wasn't a quitter, but she really *had* exhausted every possibility she *or* Georgie could think of.

What if she called Phoebe Lancaster? Maybe Joanna could talk the reporter into doing a feature spread on her and her designs, kind of a follow-up to the story about Cornelia's wedding.

But really, what good would that do? Sure, it would be nice to have a bit of publicity, but without a collection to show and somewhere to show it, what was the point?

No, Joanna might as well face it. If something good didn't happen soon, Joanna might as well pack it in and forget about her dreams. Because right now, the way things were, she had about as much chance of becoming an Oscar-winning actress as she did a successful fashion designer.

"Corny, dearest, I thought you'd decided to stay out of the matchmaking business."

Cornelia frowned. "Whatever do you mean? I'm just trying to give Joanna a leg up, that's all."

"And when you decided to call him, it never entered your mind that she and Marcus Barlow might make a nice couple?" Harry said disbelievingly.

"No, of course not." And it honestly hadn't. But now that Harry mentioned it, she couldn't help thinking how nice it would be if that lovely young man *should* like Joanna and vice versa, because Joanna was a terrific person, just the sort of spunky, strong young woman Cornelia admired.

"Knowing how romantic you are, I find that hard to believe."

"Well, believe it. When I called Marcus, the only thing on my mind—other than inviting him to dinner—was securing a show for Joanna at his gallery." Cornelia had already decided she was going to help Joanna financially, too. She had it all planned. She would arrange for Joanna to have a "loan" through the Queen Anne Community Bank in Cornelia's old neighborhood, where she had banked for years. The money would actually come directly out of Cornelia's account, but Joanna wouldn't have to know that. Just as she wouldn't have to know about Cornelia's call to Marcus.

"What are you smiling about?" Harry said, drawing

her closer. The two of them were sitting in front of the fire and enjoying their predinner cocktail.

"Oh, I was just thinking how much like you I'm becoming."

Harry grinned and nuzzled her neck. "Really?" he murmured. "In that case, I hope you've chosen one of my better qualities to emulate."

"I don't think deviousness is a better quality, but sometimes it's very useful."

Harry laughed out loud. "So you admit you're devious? Never thought I'd see the day."

"Everyone is devious once in a while. Especially for a good cause."

"The end justifies the means, in other words."

"Well…" Cornelia hated to admit when Harry was right. Better to keep him guessing.

"Now, c'mon, Corny. Be fair."

Cornelia took a sip of her Bellini, then set it down. She shivered as Harry's arms tightened around her. Turning to face him, she murmured, "I guess I could be persuaded."

As his lips met hers, she decided it wasn't so bad admitting you were wrong when the reward was so deliciously sweet.

Chapter Three

Joanna was still pinching herself. It was more than eight hours since she'd received the call that had the potential to change her life, and she still could hardly believe it.

Marcus Barlow had called her! He was interested in meeting her! He liked her designs! Yes, yes, yes!

She knew she was even thinking in exclamation points, but she couldn't seem to help herself. Truly, if—after meeting her—he agreed to give her a venue to show her collection, her life would be totally different from what it was today.

Having a show at Up and Coming and all that would entail would put JS Designs on the map. Literally on the map. If she caught the eye of the right people, if they liked her work and ordered her designs, she would be able to do all the things she'd only dreamed about doing: rent a proper workroom, with not only a place to create her designs, but a place to display them and to sell them. Ideally, there would be enough room for her to both live *and* work.

And once she had the promise of a show at Up and Coming, she could go back to the various banks. Surely, with the show in her future, someone would be willing to lend her operating capital.

Grateful that Chick the Rat was still out of town and she didn't have to take a sick day to have enough time to meet with Marcus Barlow, Joanna began getting her things ready for her eleven-thirty appointment. She was just about to leave for the gallery when her cell phone rang.

She frowned at the display. Queen Anne Community Bank? Why were *they* calling her? Thinking it was probably some kind of credit card offer, she almost let the call go to voice mail, but she had a few minutes, so she might as well answer and get rid of them. Otherwise, they'd just pester her again.

Seven minutes later, in stunned disbelief, she disconnected the call. *Holy cow!* She hoped she'd made sense in her conversation with the loan officer. What on earth was going on? Was the entire world tilting on its axis? Why else would everything suddenly make a 180-degree swing and begin to go right for her when yesterday everything in her life had been totally hopeless? It was almost as if some fairy godmother had waved a magic wand, she thought in dazed disbelief.

Queen Anne Community Bank had decided to lend her the money she needed to finance her collection. Actually, the loan they'd proposed would be enough to keep her in operating capital for a year or more. It would enable her to find a place to do business and to hire as many employees as she needed to assist her in fulfilling future orders. She'd also be able to purchase all necessary materials and equipment to run the business.

She was so excited she wasn't sure she trusted herself to drive to the gallery. Maybe, just this once, she'd indulge herself and take a taxi.

Thirty minutes later, as her watch showed it to be 11:22, the cab pulled up in front of Up and Coming. Joanna had dressed carefully for this interview. She'd worn her most demure black dress—a long-sleeved lightweight ribbed wool turtleneck that ended a modest three inches above her knees—sheer black tights and four-inch-high black suede platforms. She'd even considered removing her black nail polish, but couldn't bear to ruin her manicure, which she'd gotten Saturday and could ill afford. Dangling silver earrings and an armload of silver bangle bracelets completed her outfit, and she'd even managed to tame her unruly black hair into some semblance of a plain pixie without spikes.

The only thing worrying Joanna right now—other than actually securing the show—was the prospect of having to work with Brenda Garfield. The woman had made no secret of the way she felt about either Joanna or her designs, had she? So even if Marcus Barlow liked Joanna's work and agreed to give her the show, if the Garfield woman wasn't on board, she could make life difficult.

Worse, she could ruin the show.

Well, Joanna would just have to make sure that didn't happen. She'd worked her butt off for another chance at the brass ring. And now that it was here, she intended to grab it and hold on to it for dear life, because nothing—not Brenda Garfield, not Ivan Klemenko, not Chick, not anyone or anything—was going to take it away from her.

Not this time.

Marcus was looking forward to meeting Joanna Spinelli. From her designs, and from Cornelia Hunt's glowing recommendation, he figured he knew what to expect. He pictured a slim, elegant young woman, someone refined, with delicate features and classic beauty. She would be the kind of woman who could wear the lovely clothing she designed and do justice to it. He imagined someone modest and old-fashioned— the kind of woman he continually hoped to meet but never seemed to. Someone the exact opposite of Amanda Warren, his most recent relationship, which had ended badly.

So when Joanna Spinelli walked into the gallery just before eleven-thirty, he thought she was a sales-person...or a customer. Yes, a customer. Salespeople generally dressed more conservatively than the young woman approaching the counter.

"Hello, Miss Garfield," the woman was saying. "I'm here for my eleven-thirty appointment with Mr. Barlow."

Marcus, who stood just out of sight behind a latticework screen, stared, finding it hard to believe that this woman, who was the polar opposite of the kind of woman he'd pictured, was the designer of those beautiful clothes.

Brenda looked in his direction. "Marcus," she said.

Still in disbelief, Marcus walked out from behind the screen. "Good morning. I'm Marcus Barlow."

"Good morning. Joanna Spinelli." Her dark eyes met his.

In them, he saw intelligence and intensity. They shook hands. Her handshake was firm and strong. His initial disappointment at the way she looked faded, to be replaced by a mixture of curiosity and something else, something very close to admiration, even though she was not the type of woman who normally appealed to him. In her, though, he recognized a worthy opponent. The thought startled him. Why think of her as an opponent? If things went well today, they would be colleagues.

And he did want them to go well, even though up to this moment he hadn't been one hundred percent sure of that. "Shall we go into my office?"

Once they were settled in the office—him behind the desk, her seated in front of it, with her portfolio on the desk between them—he said, "I was impressed by the designs on your website, Ms. Spinelli."

"Thank you. But please, call me Joanna."

She should smile more often; it made her seem warmer. "And I'm Marcus." She really was quite attractive, once you got past all that black eyeliner and mascara and the dark red lipstick. Not to mention the black nail polish.

Even Vanessa knew better than to wear black nail polish in his presence. He did notice that Joanna's nails were quite short. He figured she kept them that way because it made it easier for her to work with the delicate fabrics she seemed to favor in her designs. "Before we discuss a possible show for you, I have some questions."

"Of course."

"First of all, how many designs have you ready to show?"

"Right now I have nine completed and the tenth about half done. But I've only recently found out that a business loan I applied for has been granted, so I'm planning to give notice at my day job in the morning. Once I'm working on the collection full-time, I should be able to get half a dozen more designs ready by, say, the first of November."

"I know very little about the fashion industry, but sixteen seems like a good number for a show."

"It's actually more than most designers show. I had been hoping for twelve designs. So if you feel sixteen is too many, having a couple extra would give us more options to choose from."

He nodded. "If I may ask, where are you getting a business loan?" He hoped it wasn't from some fly-by-night finance company that would gouge her.

"From the Queen Anne Community Bank."

"Really?" He couldn't keep the surprise out of his voice. Queen Anne Community Bank was one of the most conservative banks around. Joanna's hardly seemed like the kind of business they would be willing to back. They generally wanted something physical they could use as collateral against default, like a building or expensive equipment. What would she have? A few sewing machines?

"I know," she said, her own voice echoing his disbelief. "I can still hardly believe it myself. They just called me, right before I left to come here. I was shocked. I—I've been turned down everywhere. In fact, I'd given up hope." She made a face. "I probably shouldn't be telling you this."

He liked her better because she had. After all, anyone with an ounce of business sense would know she wasn't a good financial risk. No artist was.

"That answers another important question," Marcus said. "I was curious about how you've been financing your work."

"It's been tough. Up till now, I've had to squeeze

every penny out of my personal finances. Although my family has helped out some." She smiled again. "In particular, my grandmother. She believes in me. Well, actually, my entire family believes in me. But they're not wealthy. Besides, this is my dream. I knew going into it I would have to work really hard and probably have to sacrifice a lot if I was going to make it. I didn't expect anything less."

Marcus studied her thoughtfully. He was surprised to find he liked her. She seemed to have a common-sense approach to her work and a good, level head. "You might have noticed that we are planning to show the work of a young jewelry designer sometime soon."

She nodded. "Truthfully? That's the reason I thought about approaching you. When I read about the jewelry designs."

"How would you feel about our combining the two shows? Having some of the jewelry worn by your models."

She frowned. "I don't know. Um, what kind of jewelry is it? I know the designer is your sister. Miss Garfield told me. But she didn't say anything about the jewelry itself."

"I have some photos." He got up and walked to the bookcase, where he took down a thin album. He laid it in front of her and watched her face as she turned the pages and studied the various designs.

"I like them a lot," she said, finally looking up. "She makes exactly the kinds of things I like to wear, but do you really think they're compatible with my designs? I mean, the jewelry is ultrasleek, and my designs are completely the opposite."

"I think that's exactly why they'll look good together. Because they're so unexpected a combination."

She hesitated. "I don't know. I told myself I would agree to anything you suggested, but I'm just not sure this will work. Is...this a deal breaker?"

He was a bit taken aback that she hadn't immediately agreed with his suggestion. And yet he couldn't help respecting the fact that she wasn't afraid to stand up for herself. "Not necessarily. I would like for you and my sister to meet so you can see her work in person. Can you reserve judgment until then?"

She nodded, but he could see the doubt remaining in her eyes. No problem. He'd change her mind. Most people, even if they disagreed with him initially, came around to his way of thinking. "Good. We'll see if we can set something up for next week. Perhaps lunch one day? Would that work for you?"

"That sounds perfect."

He had planned to show her the work of the artist whose paintings would be featured throughout the month of November to see how she felt about being paired with him, but now he decided to wait until she and Vanessa met. He wasn't really worried about the outcome of the meeting—he was confident he could convince both women his idea was a good one—but it paid to be cautious.

"Um, Mr. Barlow...Marcus...what if, after meeting your sister, I would still prefer not to be paired with her?"

She had guts, he'd give her that. "You mean, will I still be interested in giving you a show?"

She nodded.

"Yes, I will."

"So it'll be my decision?"

He almost laughed. She definitely had guts. He was right to imagine her as an opponent earlier. "Yes. It'll be your decision. In fact, I'll ask my assistant to draw up a contract today and call you when it's ready."

Business concluded, he escorted her out to the gallery floor and watched her leave. Why all the black? he wondered. Was she trying to make some kind of statement? If so, in his opinion, it was the wrong one. But he wasn't worried about that, either. They had plenty of time to work on changing her look.

"So you sent her packing?" Brenda said once the door closed behind her.

Marcus's head shot around. He'd almost forgotten Brenda was there. "Sent her packing? No. I liked her, and I like her designs. If everything works out, I plan to give her a show."

Brenda's eyes narrowed. "I think that's a mistake, Marcus."

"And why is that?"

"Because she's hardly the type of person you want to promote."

"Her designs are beautiful."

"They're pretty enough, but I question her taste level."

"Her taste level? What do you mean?"

"Well, just look at her. I'd expect to find someone like her behind a makeup counter in one of the department stores, not here, in a gallery like ours."

"That's easily fixed."

She looked as if she wanted to continue to argue with him. Instead, she said, "Who were you thinking of pairing her with?"

"I'm not sure." He was, but he wasn't in the mood to share the information with Brenda just yet, especially since she'd obviously taken a dislike to Joanna.

"Well," she said stiffly, "I still think you're making a mistake. I also think you're setting a precedent that you will regret."

"You could be right, but we'll have to agree to disagree this time."

He turned to walk back into the office when she muttered, "I just hope you don't expect *me* to introduce her to prospective buyers."

Marcus stopped and just looked at her. Her head was bent over some papers, and even though he knew she knew he was looking at her, she didn't look up. After a few seconds, Marcus continued into the office without saying anything more. Because he knew if he did, it would be something he might be sorry for later.

"So, how'd the meeting at the gallery go today?"

"Except for the fact that I don't think Marcus Barlow likes me, it went fairly well." Joanna explained about Marcus Barlow's sister and her jewelry designs. "We're having lunch together sometime next week to see how we get on."

"Then what you said doesn't make a lick of sense," Georgie said. "If he didn't like you, he would have shown you the door today."

"That's not necessarily true."

"Why on earth do you think he doesn't like you?"

"The way he looked at me, for one thing. It was obvious he disapproved of me."

"Joanna, come on. You're exaggerating, surely."

"No, I'm not. I'm used to that look. Men either want

to get me into bed or turn up their noses when they see me. There's seldom a happy medium. And men like Marcus Barlow belong to the latter group. I'm surprised he even wants to give me a show."

"Oh, for heaven's sake. Why would how you look have any bearing on his decision to give you a show? It's your *designs* that will be shown, not you. I mean, I've seen the way some of the big-name designers look, and trust me, a lot of them are downright weird."

"Yes, but this isn't New York or Paris. This is Seattle."

"Seattle's not a cow town, you know. It's considered very hip and cool."

"By the people who live here, maybe."

"Now you're not making any sense at all. I can't imagine that a man who would own a gallery like Up and Coming would be bothered because you look more avant-garde than conservative. Anyway, we could argue about this all day and get nowhere. So let's move on. Tell me what he's like—other than the fact that you think he doesn't like you or approve of you."

"In a nutshell, he's handsome, arrogant and used to telling people what to do."

"*Arrogant?* Really?"

"Really."

"That's funny."

"What's funny?"

"My mother said he was charming. She really liked him. And she's a good judge of character."

"What do you mean, your mother said he was charming? When did you talk to your mother about him?"

"I, uh…"

"Georgie, did your mother have anything to do with him calling me?"

"Well, I, um, may have mentioned something to her about him and the gallery and how you wanted to have a show there."

"Georgie!"

"Jeez, Joanna, don't get all worked up. It's normal in the business world to use your contacts. Why shouldn't you? Anyway, I don't know if my mother called him or not. Didn't you say he said something about getting your business card from that manager of his?"

"Yes, but—"

"Well, maybe he never talked to Mom. But even if he did, it's not a big deal. He would never offer to give you a show unless he liked your work."

"Maybe *that's* why he wants to combine his sister's work with mine. Maybe he thinks mine needs help."

"I would think," Georgie said, "if he wants to show your work along with his sister's, that he really *loves* your work. I mean, his *sister,* Joanna."

"I told him I wasn't sure I wanted to have my models wearing her jewelry."

"You did? Really?"

"Yep."

Georgie laughed. "I can't believe you sometimes. And what did he say to that?" She was still laughing.

"He said it would be my decision."

"Then I have no idea what you're worried about! Sounds to me like he was perfectly reasonable and nice to you."

Joanna sighed. "On one level, I know you're right. But on another, I just have this feeling."

"What feeling?"

"That as far as my show is concerned, Marcus Barlow is going to want to have everything his way. And I'm not sure his way is my way. In fact, I'm sure it's not."

For a moment, Georgie didn't say anything. When she did, Joanna could tell she was trying not to laugh again. "Sounds to me like there might be fireworks ahead."

Joanna just hoped she wouldn't be the one getting burned.

Chapter Four

"But, Marcus, I thought this was going to be *my* chance. I don't want to share my show with someone else."

Marcus had figured Vanessa wouldn't be any more eager to share a show than Joanna had been, but his sister wasn't really in any position to argue the point, not after her behavior last week.

"This isn't fair," she cried. "You're just doing this to punish me because you're still mad at me. You grounded me all weekend! Isn't that enough?"

"I am not punishing you. Besides, combining the two shows isn't cast in stone. If, after you meet her and see her designs, you still feel you don't want to do a show with her, we'll keep them separate. But I think combining the two will enhance the work of both of you, and I'd like you to consider it."

"But I don't have to do it if I don't want to?"

"As I told Miss Spinelli, no, it'll be your decision. Yours and hers."

"So she's not any more eager to combine shows than I am?" Her eyes brightened.

"She's keeping an open mind. Now, will you take a look at her designs?"

Vanessa sighed. "Oh, all right, I'll go look at her website now."

Half an hour later, she came into the study where he was going over the household accounts. "Okay, I went to her website. And she does design beautiful clothes. They're not the kinds of things I would ever want to wear, but I can see how they'd appeal to a lot of girls. Still, I don't think—"

"They're the kinds of things you *should* wear," Marcus said, interrupting. He gave a disparaging glance at her torn jeans and tight, layered T-shirts. At five nine and a half, with her wheat-colored hair and beautiful eyes, Vanessa would be striking in one of Joanna's elegant ensembles. In fact, the dark blue evening gown overlaid in lace would look great on her. Not that she ever went to the kinds of places a young woman would wear something like that. It was all he could do to get her to attend charity functions sponsored by the family. Vanessa gave him a long-suffering look. "As I started to say, I don't think my jewelry and her designs would look good together."

"And I think the contrast between them would be interesting."

"Oh, c'mon, Marcus. You don't know anything *about* fashion. Her clothes cry out for high-end jewels, the kinds of things made by Neil Lane or Harry Winston." She rolled her eyes to show what she thought of *them*.

"Most young women would kill to be able to wear high-end jewels," he said mildly.

"I'm not like everyone else."

Where had this rebellious streak come from? Until recently, Vanessa had been one of the most agreeable sisters imaginable. In fact, she would have done just about anything to please him. But lately she seemed to delight in opposing him. "I only want you to meet the woman."

"But what's the point?"

"The point is, I've asked it as a favor to me."

If looks could kill, hers was lethal. "Oh, whatever. Fine. I'll meet her."

"Good."

"When?"

"We'll go to lunch with her one day early next week."

"I have a really busy week coming up."

"One lunch won't take up that much of your time."

Marcus put his head in his hands after Vanessa, with another elaborate sigh and still grumbling under her breath, left the room. Why couldn't people just be reasonable? It was a good thing this day was nearly over. Between the problems he'd had this morning with a new supplier in Copenhagen, Brenda's almost insubordination after the meeting with Joanna Spinelli, and Vanessa's pouts and sighs, he was ready for something different.

Unfortunately, he still had dinner with his mother to look forward to. And with the way his luck was running, she'd have a list of problems she expected him to solve.

Sometimes Marcus just wanted to throw in the towel. Pack a bag and take off for parts unknown.

But he wouldn't do that, would he?

No, because unlike the women in his life, Marcus didn't shirk his responsibilities. He'd accepted his path long ago, and he'd follow it to the bitter end. There were no deal breakers for him.

Although Joanna could hardly wait to give her notice, there was no way she was giving up her day off, so it was Friday morning before she could tell Chick the news.

"Hey, babe," he said when he sauntered in at ten. Chick was *not* an early riser.

"I'm not your babe, Chick." She tossed the empty container from her breakfast of blackberry yogurt into the trash can.

"Ah, come on." He smiled down at her. "No hard feelings. We're still friends, aren't we?"

Joanna gave him a look. Friends. What was it with some guys? Did they think they could do anything and you'd still slobber over them? She'd be willing to bet he still believed she'd forget how he'd treated her and jump into the sack with him if he acted the way he wanted her to. "I don't think we were ever friends," she muttered.

He acted as if he hadn't heard her and was already heading into his office.

"There's an important letter sitting on your desk," she called after him.

Less than two minutes later, he came stomping out, brandishing the letter, an expression of stunned astonishment on his face. "You're *quitting?*"

She smiled sweetly, tamping down the urge to say, *Can't you read English?* "Yes, I am."

"You can't be serious."

"I'm deadly serious."

"Oh, come on, Joanna. I thought we were past all that."

Joanna sighed. "Chick, this is not about you and me. It's about me finally getting the chance to do what I've always wanted to do."

"What are you talking about?"

"I'm going to be a full-time fashion designer from now on."

"And you think you can support yourself doing *that*?"

Joanna had always known he didn't take her aspirations seriously, and his attitude this morning proved it. "Don't worry about me. I'll be just fine." Earlier this morning she wasn't sure if she would tell him about her upcoming show or not. Now she decided he didn't deserve to know. Let him be shocked when he read about it in the paper or saw it covered on the local news. "Do you want me to call the employment agency or do you want to do it?"

He stared at her. "You're really quitting."

She nodded. "Afraid so."

"Fine," he sputtered, "but you can forget about this two-weeks bull. You can't leave until we can find someone else and you can get her trained, no matter how long it takes."

"I'm sorry, Chick, but that's not the way it works. Two weeks' notice is all I'm required to give you." She almost felt sorry for him. But not sorry enough to give him any more of her precious time than she absolutely had to. After all, it wasn't as if she needed a reference. She had no intention of ever working at anything but designing clothes again. Besides, knowing him, he would drag his feet forever without a reason not to.

"But that may not be enough time." Now he sounded panicky. "What if I can't find someone right away?"

"In that case, I guess you'll just have to use a temp."

"A temp? Are you crazy?"

Now it was her turn to stare at him.

Finally he said, "Okay. Okay. Call the agency. And be sure to tell them it's urgent. Christ, this is the worst possible time of year for you to do this to me."

Ignoring his grumbling, she said, "What shall I tell the agency about salary?"

He named a figure a good ten percent higher than he was currently paying her. She figured he did it just to piss her off. But she decided not to give him the satisfaction. "I'll call them right now."

Half an hour later, she was in the midst of relaying to Chick what the agency had had to say when her cell phone rang. Seeing *Barlow International* on the caller ID, she said, "Excuse me, Chick. I have to take this call."

"Miss Spinelli?" the caller said. "This is Judith Holmes. I'm Mr. Barlow's assistant. He asked me to tell you he has your contract ready and wondered if you could meet him at the gallery sometime this afternoon."

"The only time I could come would be after work. But I quit at four on Fridays, so I could be there by five o'clock." The gallery stayed open until six on weeknights.

"I'm sure that'll be fine. If there's a problem, I'll call you back. Otherwise, just plan to be there then."

"Thank you."

Chick was glaring at her when she hung up. "Since you're only giving me two weeks' notice, all personal calls will be off-limits from now on."

She felt like telling him where to put it, that if he was going to act like this, she would just pack up her things and go now. But the urge didn't last long. She wasn't looking for all-out warfare. Besides, Chick could blow hot air all day long, and he could establish all the rules he wanted, but the bottom line was, he didn't spend enough time in the office to enforce rules about phone calls or anything else.

Oh, revenge was sweet.

For the rest of the day, Joanna couldn't stop smiling.

Marcus generally let Brenda take care of getting the gallery contracts signed, but because she was so negative about Joanna and her work, he had decided he would meet with Joanna instead. He could kill two birds that way: get the contract taken care of and introduce Joanna to the work of Jamison Wells, see what she thought of it.

When he called Brenda to tell her, she said, "There's no reason for you to make a special trip, Marcus. Just messenger the contract over. I can take care of it. I do it all the time."

"I'll be over in that direction anyway," he said, "so it's no problem. Besides, there are some additional things I want to discuss with Miss Spinelli." He could tell Brenda wanted to say something else, but she didn't. The truth was, he didn't trust her where Joanna was concerned. In fact, he wouldn't put it past her to do or say something that would cause Joanna to change her mind.

And for some reason Marcus couldn't explain, he didn't want that to happen.

* * *

Joanna had been going to make a quick stop home to change clothes before going to the gallery, but after thinking it over, she decided going straight from work would be a good test of Georgie's theory that the way she looked had no significance when it came to her show. So when she walked into Up and Coming at four forty-five that afternoon, she was still wearing what she'd put on that morning: a black velvet miniskirt paired with a black silk long-sleeved T-shirt, shimmery silver tights and her favorite high-button shoe boots. She also wore mismatched silver earrings—on the right ear, a huge starburst, on the other a long dangle of zodiac signs. Too bad her tattoo wasn't visible, she thought with an inner grin. That would *really* test his mettle.

She almost laughed out loud when she saw Brenda Garfield's expression. The woman looked as if she'd just bitten into a sour lemon. "I'll tell Marcus you're here," she said.

To Marcus's credit, the only indication he gave that her appearance was in any way startling was a slight widening of his eyes—quickly checked—when he walked onto the gallery floor and saw her. Smiling, he said, "Come on into the office. I've got the contract ready."

Too bad he was so not her type, because he was undeniably sexy with that thick dark hair of his and those cool blue-gray eyes. Today he even seemed less *CEO* and more *GQ,* in fawn slacks, a creamy cashmere sweater and a wool jacket the color of espresso. And she had to admit it; he'd gone up a notch in her estimation by not reacting to today's outfit. She'd love to know what he was thinking, though, because she was sure he'd much rather she was dressed like Brenda, who today wore a tailored crepe dress in a deep shade of plum.

"I never asked you where you worked when we talked the other day," he said once they were alone.

"My boss is a wine merchant. He travels all over the area buying and selling wine, and I run the office. We also do a lot of internet sales." Joanna was particularly proud of that, because it had been her idea to go after the internet trade—which Chick had never given her credit for. Shades of Ivan the Terrible Klemenko. Man, Georgie was right, she *did* have bad judgment when it came to men.

"How long have you worked there?" Marcus asked.

"A little over six years."

"I'll bet your boss is sorry to see you go. I know I'd be up a creek if my assistant left."

Joanna simply nodded. She didn't want to get into a discussion of Chick. She didn't trust herself not to say something derogatory.

They chatted a few more minutes; then Marcus handed Joanna her contract, and she carefully looked it over. But as she'd expected, the terms were simple and reasonable. By signing the papers, she would be agreeing that in return for having a show at Up and Coming, which would include all advertising and promotion, she would pay five percent of any resulting sales back to the gallery.

"How will 'resulting sales' be determined?" she asked.

"You'll be on the honor system," Marcus said.

Joanna knew her face reflected her shock. The honor system? How could the gallery do business that way?

"I know what you're thinking," he said. "But I never expected to make much money off the gallery. I do what I do to help struggling artists. And, as far as I know, no one who's had work shown at the gallery has ever cheated me."

"Well, I'm amazed. Most businessmen…and women… are a lot less trusting."

"When it comes to Barlow International, so am I." He smiled. "The truth is, the gallery is an indulgence for me. When I was younger, I studied art, wanted to be an artist myself. That didn't work out, so this is the way I compensate and keep my hand in the game."

The great Marcus Barlow had wanted to be an artist? Suddenly Joanna saw him in an entirely different light. She was dying to know why it hadn't worked out, but it was obvious he didn't intend to elaborate.

"I don't expect you to sign the contract now," he said instead. "Take it home so you can study it. In fact, you can have a lawyer look it over, if you like."

"That won't be necessary. I'm happy to sign it today."

"Even though you won't meet my sister until next week?"

"Even though." So saying, she signed both copies, and then he did the same.

Handing her one of the copies, he said, "Now, if you've got time, I want to show you the work of the artist we've booked for the month of November. I think your work would look particularly good with his."

Walking over to a large bookcase, he removed a portfolio and brought it back to the desk. This time, he didn't sit across from her. Instead, he pulled a side chair over so they could both look at the portfolio together. Joanna caught the faint scent of a woodsy cologne as he settled next to her.

The moment he opened the portfolio and she saw the photo of the first painting, she was mesmerized. The painting, which depicted a small boy chasing a ball, was a cross between an abstract and something more realistic, using a wide spectrum of vivid colors.

As he continued to slowly turn the pages, she saw that each painting featured at least one person. There were no landscapes, no still lifes and no "big" scenes. She particularly loved a painting that showed a young woman sitting on a park bench. It was done in shades of blue and green, with deft touches of purple in the background. Joanna could just see one of her dresses, a violet crocheted number, displayed nearby. The two, dress and painting, would enhance each other.

Another painting, this one featuring an old woman feeding a squirrel against a background that looked like dunes, was done in bold shades of gold, ochre and russet.

Delighted, she turned to Marcus. "I love them! I was so afraid you'd pick an artist who works in pastels or something—you know, faux impressionists."

"And I was afraid you wouldn't see the advantage of the contrast between Wells's spare art and your designs."

"His paintings are the perfect foil for my work, I think."

"So do I," Marcus said.

"What kind of style is this? It's almost realistic, but not quite."

"It's called painterly. You'll notice that the artist hasn't tried to conceal his brushstrokes or technique, and that the style celebrates the use of color."

"Well, I love what he's done. It's wonderful."

"He's the most promising artist I've seen in a long time. We're really looking forward to his show and expect to attract a lot of potential buyers. Which will benefit you, too, of course."

If Joanna hadn't realized before just how lucky she was to have this opportunity, she certainly did now. "You know, I don't think I've really thanked you properly for what you're doing for me. I just want you to know that I'm very grateful to have this opportunity."

"And I'm pleased to be able to provide it."

Oh, wow. That smile of his was definitely dangerous. Her heart skittered a little as their eyes met, and something arced between them. *Whoa. What was that?* But Joanna knew what it was. She was experienced enough to know that what she was feeling was a very strong sexual attraction, and she was pretty sure Marcus felt the same vibe. Too bad, she thought regretfully. Sexual vibe or not, her relationship with Marcus Barlow was never going to be anything but a business one. Because no matter how attractive he was and no matter how sexy, he was so far from being the kind of man who held any promise for her that they might as well be on different planets.

Marcus Barlow represented old money and the upper echelons of Seattle society, whereas Joanna was from a blue-collar family and even though someday she'd love to be rich and famous, she had no desire to desert her class.

In fact, she loved her class. Even her friendship

with Georgie and the glimpses she'd had into Georgie's more privileged life had shown Joanna that the way she'd been raised—even when she chafed against it—had given her something valuable, something she cherished.

I am who I am, she thought, *and I've never wanted to be anything different.*

Marcus closed the portfolio and stood. "I have two of Wells's paintings in the storeroom. Come on, I'll show them to you."

As they walked out into the gallery, Brenda looked around. There was an expression on her face that was almost venomous, although she quickly smoothed it out. Joanna realized Brenda was seething. Maybe there was more to her dislike of Joanna than Joanna had first thought. Maybe the woman had designs on Marcus and saw Joanna as competition. This amused Joanna, because it didn't take a rocket scientist to see that, like herself, Brenda wasn't in his class, either. *No, honey,* she wanted to say, *you're wasting your time. Neither of us is in his ballpark, I'm afraid.*

"I'm taking Miss Spinelli back to see those two paintings of Jamison Wells," Marcus said.

"Oh?" Brenda walked over to where they were standing. "Are you thinking of showing her designs during his exhibition here?" Her dark blue eyes turned as icy as the Arctic.

Even though Joanna could hardly stand the woman, she couldn't help feeling sorry for Brenda. Her unhappiness was so obvious, and the reason for it even more obvious. After all, if Joanna, who didn't know her at all, could figure out its origin, surely Marcus could.

Then again, most men, even the smartest men, were totally clueless when it came to relationships.

"Yes, I think so," he said. "Joanna likes his work very much, and agrees with me that it will be a great pairing with hers."

If Joanna had thought Brenda's original expression had been venomous, then the look in her eyes now was nothing short of murderous. She was glad that Marcus didn't continue the conversation and instead headed toward the back of the gallery and a door that led to the storeroom.

Marcus went in, switched on the overhead light, stepped aside to allow Joanna to enter the room then closed the door behind him. Why had he done that? She couldn't help thinking of that earlier strong sexual vibe between them. She wondered what on earth Brenda was thinking now. Although Joanna knew she was being silly to think the closed door had some kind of significance, her heart didn't get the message and picked up speed.

"I've got his paintings over there, by the wall," Marcus said. He smiled. "Out of harm's way."

His perfectly normal smile even caused a tiny flurry of butterflies in her stomach. She almost rolled her eyes at herself. What was her problem? Telling herself to get real and remember the reason she was here, which had nothing to do with sex, she followed his lead.

Between the doorway and the indicated wall were filing cabinets, a couple of rows of shelves filled with supplies, about a dozen stackable chairs, and any number of assorted pieces of furniture and equipment. These all created a division between the doorway and the paintings, which were all loosely covered in a soft cloth. She looked around with interest because in addition to the covered paintings, there were several sculptures in the same area that she'd like to see a bit closer.

"Another artist we're considering giving a show," Marcus said, seeing her interest.

She nodded, fascinated by everything in the room. Including the way-too-attractive man standing only feet away. The one who had just removed the covering from the first painting. The one again smiling at her. And, oh, her idiotic heart was so not listening to her!

She stepped forward so she could see the painting better—the light wasn't great in the room, there was only one window and the one overhead fixture—but instead of looking at the painting, her eyes met Marcus's. He dropped his hand from the painting and his gaze moved to her mouth. At the same time, he took a step toward her.

He was going to kiss her!

The realization stunned her. She could hardly breathe. She couldn't have moved if her life depended upon it.

"Joanna…" he said, his voice little more than a gruff whisper. He reached out as Joanna swayed forward.

And…at that very moment…just as Joanna's eyes drifted shut and her lips actually tingled in anticipation of his, the door to the storeroom opened noisily and Brenda said, "Marcus, Jamison Wells is on the phone. Do you—" She broke off abruptly as Marcus and Joanna both jumped.

There were only about two seconds of awkward silence before Marcus said—coolly, no less, "Tell him I'll call him back later. Probably not until tonight."

"But he said—"

"I'll call him back later, Brenda." This time Marcus's tone left no room for argument.

"Fine," Brenda said and walked out. She left the door open.

Joanna wasn't sure whether she was glad Brenda had interrupted or disappointed. But she couldn't think about that now. She had to pull herself together and remember she was a professional person and she was here on business, not pleasure. And yet…

But she broke off the thought because Marcus had lifted the first of the two paintings he wanted her to see and walked toward the window where the late afternoon sun had provided a pool of natural light. Although it was hard to pretend nothing had happened, even though nothing actually had happened, Joanna forced herself to concentrate on the work of Jamison Wells and not the nearness and butterfly-inducing closeness of Marcus Barlow.

After they'd looked at the two paintings, which Joanna loved even more than she'd loved the photographs because now she could see the brushwork and the richness of the colors, they walked back out to the gallery.

"Thank you for everything," she said, aware Brenda was listening to every word.

"You're very welcome," he said.

Still acutely conscious of Brenda and feeling awkward anyway, Joanna said, "Well, I guess I'd better be going."

"Did you drive over?" Marcus asked.

"No, I walked."

"Do you need a—"

"Marcus, you're not planning to leave yet, are you?" Brenda asked, interrupting.

He frowned. "I was thinking about it, yes."

"I need you to look at some letters of inquiry that came in this week."

"Can't they wait until Monday? I—"

"No. I think we need to act on one or two of them quickly."

"I don't want to keep you any longer," Joanna said hurriedly.

He sounded resigned as he answered. "We'll have a chance to talk more next week. I'll give you a call to let you know where and when."

"I'm looking forward to it." Joanna didn't dare look at Brenda. She could only imagine what the other woman was thinking about this last exchange.

As Joanna walked away from the gallery, she guessed she'd never know what he had been planning to ask her before Brenda stopped him. Maybe he was simply going to offer her a ride home. But what if he'd wanted more? What if he'd decided to act upon that sexual attraction that had so quickly risen between them? What if a ride home had morphed into a dinner invitation? And then a real kiss? And possibly even more.

Well, whatever his intention had been, it was best that he'd been thwarted. Because Marcus Barlow was dangerous with a capital *D*. She must always bear that in mind. He belonged to a different world, one she could never fit into.

Chick might have been a poor choice because he was her boss...and a jerk, as it turned out, but Marcus Barlow would be an impossible choice. Totally impossible. Anything other than a business relationship with him would be a fast train to heartache.

And she'd better never forget that.

Chapter Five

By the time Marcus finished looking at the letters of inquiry from artists interested in showing their work at Up and Coming, Joanna was long gone.

Probably a good thing, he told himself, even though before Brenda had delayed him he'd intended to offer Joanna a ride home and then, once they were on their way, suggest dinner somewhere.

He knew taking her to dinner would have been a mistake, that it would be best to keep their relationship strictly business, the way he did with all the artists he featured. He'd learned long ago it was never a good idea to mix business with pleasure. Only problems could ever come from the combination, especially when the other party happened to be a woman. Although Marcus only knew what Joanna had chosen to tell him and what he'd observed with his own eyes, he recognized danger when he saw it.

And Joanna Spinelli, she of the spiked hair, chocolate-brown eyes, sexy little body and gorgeous legs—oh, yes, he'd noticed her legs, all right—might as well have been wearing a red flag with flashing lights.

Today, when their eyes had met over Jamison Wells's paintings, Marcus knew exactly what it was that had momentarily stopped his breath and almost caused him to kiss her. And he also knew enough to steer away from it. Far away from it. Because when a person wanted more than a romp in bed, it made no sense to pursue a relationship where you had nothing in common beyond a sexual attraction. And unfortunately, Marcus and Joanna were totally different.

The two of them as a couple made no sense. For instance, unless Joanna were to change drastically, Marcus couldn't imagine ever taking her home to meet his mother. Laurette would take one look at Joanna and be appalled. Not that his mother's reaction would sway him if he believed he was making the right choice, but still…any wife of his would need to get along with his mother.

Wife? Was he really thinking of Joanna Spinelli in those terms? Had he lost his mind?

Sure, he could probably persuade Joanna to change her outward image so that it was more suited to promoting her designs. But that didn't mean she'd magically turn into the kind of woman Marcus needed in his life. Not only did he think she and his mother would never see eye to eye, but he couldn't envision her being happy running his household. And he knew instinctively she was not someone who would enjoy the philanthropic, business and social activities and responsibilities that dominated his life. She hoped to have a dynamic and thriving career of her own, one that would not be compatible with his.

For all those reasons, at this point in his life, when he was tired of relationships destined to be temporary and wanted to find someone with whom to build a future, it only made sense to stay away from Joanna. Far away.

Telling himself he had enough personal problems and didn't need more, he firmly put Joanna out of his mind. Briefly wondering if he should wait until the worst of rush-hour traffic had subsided before heading home to Washington Park, he decided to gather his briefcase and iPhone and be on his way.

He was glad tonight was free. He wasn't in the mood for any kind of obligation, social or otherwise. All he wanted was a good dinner and a drink in front of the fire, preferably in the privacy of his own apartment. He was just walking back into the gallery when his cell rang, showing Vanessa was on the line.

"Marcus," she said without preamble, "Tad's home."

Marcus swore inwardly. There went his peaceful evening. "What kind of shape is he in?"

"He seems okay. A lot quieter than usual. He's in with Mom right now."

"Thanks for letting me know. I'll be there soon."

After telling Brenda to have a good weekend, Marcus walked over to the garage where he had parked his red Ferrari 458 Italia. He deliberately didn't think about Tad or the upcoming scene until he was well on his way. Thankfully, driving had always soothed him. Even heavy traffic seemed easier to bear when he was in his much-loved car.

When he finally allowed himself to think about his brother, he wondered what excuses and promises Tad would make this time. This kind of thing—quitting something he'd promised to see through till the end— had been going on now for at least ten years, ever since Tad had just barely graduated from college, and each time Marcus hoped would be the last, that Tad would finally grow up and accept responsibility for his life.

But instead of things getting better, they seemed to be getting worse.

Marcus wondered what fresh hell he was in for tonight. He also wondered why he hadn't heard from Celia Kimball at Rosewood Rehab. She always alerted him if there was a problem. Surely they realized Tad had left the center. Or did they? It wasn't as if he'd been locked up. Rosewood prided itself on its progressive attitude toward drug addiction and the latest in treatments.

Maybe his brother had just walked out. But why? Marcus and Tad had cut a deal. Marcus would pay for Tad's treatment at Rosewood and, in turn, Tad would complete the program and get clean. Afterward Marcus would see about finding a place for Tad in the family business. Because one thing was for sure. Tad needed to work, not just because it would be good for him to become a productive part of society but because he'd run through all the discretionary money left to him by their father. The rest of Tad's fortune was tied up in the business itself, and he couldn't touch it unless he sold shares of his stock, and he couldn't do that without both Marcus's and Laurette's permission. At least their father had put that safeguard in place.

So surely Tad hadn't just walked out of Rosewood. The consequences were too dire for him to simply quit the program.

And yet…knowing Tad and how reckless he could be, nothing would really surprise Marcus. On and on his thoughts went. By the time he reached the gates of the Barlow Estate, he had the beginnings of a nasty headache. He decided to head for his own apartment first. Fortifying himself with a couple of Advil, he thought about changing clothes but decided it was better to talk to Tad first.

Back in the main house, he heard voices coming from the living room. As he approached, he told himself no matter what, he wouldn't lose his temper.

"Hello, big brother." Tad, who sat near the fireplace where a cheery fire was well under way, looked perfectly comfortable with his long legs stretched out in front of him and what looked like a half glass of red wine in his right hand.

"This is a surprise," Marcus said. He glanced over at his mother, who sat across from Tad. She, too, had a glass of wine, but hers looked barely touched. Her wary glance met Marcus's briefly. "Did you know he was coming?" he asked her.

She frowned. "No, of course not. I would have told you."

Marcus wasn't sure he believed her but decided not to press the issue. Directing his attention back to his brother, he said, "So, what brings you home, Tad?"

"I was homesick?" He smiled, obviously amused.

Marcus told himself to count to ten. "Is this something you and Mrs. Kimball discussed? Did she give her permission?"

"I don't need anyone's permission to leave."

"I know that, but you did promise me you would complete the program. Have you?"

"That promise was given before I knew how worthless the program is."

"Worthless? A program costing thirty thousand dollars for ninety days is worthless? You know yourself Rosewood came highly recommended." He wanted to add that if Tad had had to pay for the program out of his own pocket, he might not be so quick to label it worthless. But what good would that do? Tad only heard what he wanted to hear.

"I was tired of it." The amused expression had disappeared. Now Tad only looked and sounded petulant.

"Tired of it."

"Will you quit repeating everything I say?"

"It's hard not to, when what you say doesn't make any sense."

"For Christ's sake, Marcus, stop treating me like a child. I'm fine. I don't need that damn program anymore. I'm sick of being told what to do, by them *and* by you!"

Marcus felt like grabbing his brother by his expensive jacket and yanking him up out of that chair. "I see. So you're ready to get a job now? Take responsibility for yourself? Pay your own way?"

"Well, yeah, but not right this minute. I'm going to need some downtime. You know, to destress."

"Tell you what, you can destress all you want, but you're not going to live here while you do it."

"Now, Marcus..." Laurette said.

"I mean it, Mother. If Tad wants to go his own way, I think he should."

"Just because I don't want to stay in that stupid program doesn't mean I want to abandon the family!" Tad stood and drained his glass of wine. He stared at Marcus.

Marcus chuckled.

"What's so funny?" demanded Tad. His face had turned red.

"I just find it amusing how quickly you can backpedal. You don't want to be told what to do. But when

I tell you that you can make your own decisions and live any way you want to, you suddenly don't *want to abandon the family*. You really are something. Could the fact that you can't afford to be on your own have anything to do with your sudden affection for living here?"

Tad looked as if he was about to explode. "You think you're so smart, don't you?"

"I don't think I'm smart at all," Marcus said, suddenly exhausted. "I'm tired and I really have no desire to talk about this anymore tonight. Right now I plan to pour myself a drink, then go and talk to Franny." He looked at his mother again. "I'm sorry, Mother, but I'm going to have my dinner upstairs in my own apartment tonight. That way you and Tad can get caught up. And, Tad…" His gaze moved to his brother. "We'll settle this in the morning. Meet me in the dining room for breakfast at nine."

Marcus walked out without waiting for an answer.

By the time Joanna got back to the office, retrieved her car, fought rush-hour traffic and arrived home, it was nearly six-thirty. Normally, after a day like today, she'd be exhausted, ready to just plop on the couch, drink a glass of wine, watch a little TV and pet Tabitha.

But today she was too wound up to relax. She wished she had somewhere to go and someone to go with her. She could have gone clubbing with some pals—she'd been invited—but she'd turned them down. Now she was sorry.

And yet, was she really in the mood for a smoky club and a too-loud band? *Face it. You're still think-*

ing about Marcus Barlow and the almost kiss and the
dinner invitation you were hoping for.

It really was ludicrous that she felt so disappointed
not to be invited to dinner. But maybe inviting her to
dinner had never even entered his mind? She'd probably simply imagined he was attracted to her, that
he'd intended to kiss her. Anyway, what did it matter? Hadn't she already decided he was totally out of
her sphere and that she should absolutely not think of
him in that way?

Of course, it was a lot easier to tell yourself you
needed to do something than to actually do it.

She was still lecturing herself when her cell rang.
Seeing it was her mother calling, Joanna debated letting the call go to voice mail. Then again, maybe talking to her mother would be good for her. Bring her
back to reality.

"Hi, Mom," she said.

"Hi, honey. Did I get you at a bad time?"

"No. Just pouring myself a glass of wine."

"I was anxious to find out how your meeting with
Mr. Barlow went."

Since it didn't look as if Joanna was going anywhere, she put the phone on speaker and while talking to her mother changed into her oldest and most
comfortable jeans, an oversize sweater and her UGG
slippers.

"Well," her mother said when Joanna was done,
"that all sounds very promising. So, what's next?"

"Next I have to get six more designs finished. I also
need to hire someone to help me, maybe two some-
ones. And I have to find a place where I can work and
have a showroom." Good grief. It had just that moment

dawned on Joanna that she had to do all that *before* her show at the gallery. A show that was a mere eight or nine weeks away, and during two of those weeks she would barely have time to breathe, because knowing Chick, she would be working her buns off.

"But those are all such pleasurable things to do," her mother was saying as Joanna's thoughts whirled. "And I can help you. Why don't you plan to come for dinner Sunday and we can make lists? It'll be fun." There was nothing Ann Marie Spinelli enjoyed more than making lists and organizing things. She even enjoyed it when she knew Joanna's dad would probably discourage half of her ideas.

"Ohmigod, Mom," Joanna said. "Until I said everything out loud, I don't know what I was *thinking*. I can't imagine how I'll get everything done. I have to find someone to help me, like, immediately." She looked around in a panic, as if this unknown person might be somewhere in the room.

"Now, honey, calm down. I know all of this must feel a bit overwhelming, but you know what to do."

Joanna swallowed. She *did*?

Then as quickly as the panic had overtaken her, it began to subside. Of course she knew what to do. She was, after all, her mother's daughter, and she had no naysayers living with *her*. She laughed shakily. "You're right. I have to make a list and prioritize. And then just do one thing at a time."

"And I'll help you. Now…what about Sunday?"

"I should work on Sunday."

"Joanna…"

"Oh, okay. I'll come for eleven-thirty Mass and stay for dinner. But then I'm coming home to work."

"Of course. But only after we make our lists."

Joanna laughed. Her mother always managed to have the last word.

Chapter Six

Marcus was skeptical about the chance of Tad actually showing up for breakfast when he was supposed to, so he couldn't hide his surprise when he entered the main dining room and saw his brother shoveling scrambled eggs into his mouth.

"Didn't think I'd be here, did you?" Tad said when he'd finished swallowing.

"Life is full of surprises," Marcus said. He walked to the sideboard where fresh fruit and several varieties of juice waited. After pouring himself a glass of tomato juice, he sat in his customary seat at the head of the table. A carafe of hot coffee was already there.

As if some hidden bell had summoned her, Franny quietly appeared at his side. "What can I get you this morning, Mr. Marcus?"

"How about a toasted bagel?"

"Butter or cream cheese?"

"Butter and blackberry jam."

Franny smiled and nodded. Before walking away, she handed him the *Wall Street Journal* as well as the *Seattle Times*.

"So, what's the verdict?" Tad said. "Are you going to put me in chains and throw me into the dungeon?"

"Don't tempt me." Marcus drank his juice, then added cream to his coffee.

"Oh, c'mon, Marcus, it's not that bad. In fact, I'm fine. Call up Old Beagle Beak if you don't believe me."

Old Beagle Beak was the nickname Tad had given to Celia Kimball, the head of Rosewood. "I intend to."

"Good. She'll agree with me."

"If you say so." He seriously doubted this. "In the meantime, did you think about our conversation last night?"

Tad shrugged. "Yeah. I guess."

"And?"

"I haven't changed my mind, if that's what you mean. I told you. I need some time to get used to life on the outside again."

Marcus felt like saying participating voluntarily in a rehab program wasn't even close to being in prison, but what good would it do? He and Tad had had similar conversations for years. Tad saw things his own way, whether his way had any relation to reality or not.

"Tell you what," Marcus said after drinking some of his coffee. "I'll give you a month. If, at the end of that time, you haven't figured out where you're going from here, or if you haven't found a job on your own, we'll find you a spot at Barlow. Somewhere you can learn about the business from the ground up."

"Let's get something straight." Tad put down his fork and stared at Marcus. "I'm not going to work at the loading dock. If that's what you've got in mind, you can just forget about it."

"I was thinking more along the lines of shipping and receiving." That's where Marcus himself had begun.

"Just as bad," Tad muttered.

"And just what would you consider an appropriate place to begin?" Marcus told himself not to lose his temper.

Before Tad had a chance to answer, Vanessa entered the room. "Good morning," she said.

"Morning," the brothers said simultaneously. Then, turning back to Marcus, Tad said, "What does shipping have to do with accounting? I do have an accounting degree, you know."

"You've never used it."

"I did so! I worked at Turner & Turner." Turner & Turner was a local Seattle accounting firm.

"For how long?" They both knew he'd been "let go" a month after he was hired.

"So the job didn't last long. What difference does that make?"

"It makes a great deal of difference."

"You're determined to punish me, aren't you?"

"I don't consider it punishment to ask you to learn the business the way I learned it."

"I'm not you, Marcus."

"That's obvious."

Tad abruptly stood, causing several of the glasses on the table to wobble. "I can do without your sarcasm."

"But not without my money." The words were said quietly, but their effect was like a bomb bursting.

"*Your* money! *Your* money! I'm sick of hearing that from you. It's *our* money. Dad left it to all of us equally."

"Yes," Marcus said, still quietly. "He did. But he was smart enough to put safeguards in place. You've run through all the money you can legally use any way you want to. And you cannot sell your stock without both Mother's and my permission."

"That's ridiculous, and you know it. I'm thirty-two years old, for God's sake. My share of stock is worth millions, but some stupid will says I can't touch a penny of it. I'm going to hire a lawyer. See if I don't."

"You're free to do whatever you please. Just remember—I'm not going to pay for the lawyer. You'll have to find a way to do that yourself."

Since another of the terms of their father's will stipulated that once Tad's initial cash settlement—or any of theirs—was gone, they would each receive a monthly allowance of a thousand dollars and no more, Marcus knew it would be impossible for Tad to hire a lawyer until he found a job.

In answer to Marcus's proclamation, Tad slammed his hand down on the table, glared at his brother, then, muttering under his breath something about Marcus being sorry, he stomped from the room.

Vanessa, who hadn't said a word during this tirade, walked around to where Marcus sat. She leaned down and hugged him. "I'm sorry I've given you a bad time lately," she said.

Marcus squeezed her hand. "Thank you."

"He'll settle down. He's just angry right now."

"You think so?"

"I hope so, anyway."

"Do you think I'm doing the right thing?"

"Yes, I do. To allow him to sell off his stock would be a disaster."

Sometimes Marcus wasn't sure. As Tad had pointed out, he was old enough to do what he wanted with his life. And if that meant he squandered the remainder of his inheritance, why should Marcus care?

Why? Because you've had to be a grown-up your entire life. You've had to make tough decisions and take responsibility for everything and everyone, whether you wanted to or not. You don't know any other way to behave.

And if Marcus *did* allow Tad to blow the rest of his money, then what? Tad would still be an albatross around Marcus's neck, for Marcus would never let him starve.

And Tad knew that.

No wonder he wouldn't grow up.

Joanna had hoped to hear from Marcus or his assistant on Monday, but it was Tuesday before the assistant called. Thankfully, Chick was away for the day, so Joanna didn't have to worry about him overhearing the conversation and giving her grief over it.

"Miss Spinelli?"

"Yes."

"This is Judith Holmes, Mr. Barlow's assistant."

"Yes, hi."

"Mr. Barlow wanted me to ask you if you would be available to lunch with him and his sister on Thursday."

Joanna smiled. So much better to do the lunch thing on her day off than argue with Chick about how long she'd be gone. "Thursday's perfect," she said happily.

"Good. Mr. Barlow said to tell you he would stop by and pick you up at noon, if that works for you."

"Pick me up?"

"Yes, he figured that would be more convenient for

you than having to drive somewhere and find a place to park. You know how Seattle can be." The Holmes woman chuckled. "Besides, he likes to drive." Her voice lowered conspiratorially. "He has a really neat car."

Joanna smiled. "Well, in that case, great."

"He said he'll need your address."

Joanna gave it to the woman, thanked her and they hung up. Afterward, Joanna sat and looked at the phone for a long time. She had butterflies just thinking about how her life had changed in the past week. She'd gone from a person with very few options to one with a bright future ahead of her.

And all of it was due to Marcus Barlow. Well, not *all* of it. Some of her good fortune was due to the Queen Anne Community Bank and their generous loan. But the show Marcus had promised her was what would really put her and her designs on the map.

Joanna hugged herself. She was so happy right now. Everything in her life was finally going the way she'd dreamed of it going. In fact, the sky seemed to be the limit. She kept thinking it was probably a sin to be so happy. In fact, she was probably tempting fate. No doubt just daring fate to throw a monkey wrench into her plans.

She just hoped the monkey wrench wouldn't turn out to be Vanessa Barlow. Because no matter what Marcus Barlow had said, no matter that he seemed to really like her—she couldn't help thinking of that moment in the storeroom—Joanna knew it would be best if his sister liked her and her designs, too. Otherwise, there was nothing stopping Marcus from changing his mind. Contract or no contract.

* * *

Joanna hated to be late, so on Thursday, to ensure that Marcus wouldn't have to wait for her, she went down to the lobby of her building fifteen minutes before noon. While waiting, she sat and chatted with Thomas, the security guard, while keeping one eye out for Marcus's arrival.

A few minutes before noon, a sleek red sports car pulled up to the curb. Joanna had no idea what kind of car it was; she just knew it was expensive. It had to belong to Marcus. Sure enough, she'd barely pushed open the front door of her building when she saw Marcus emerge from the driver's side. He smiled when he saw her and managed to come around and open the passenger door before she even reached it.

Always the gentleman, she thought, half amused and half annoyed. The annoyance was caused by her wish to find *some* fault with him. Why did he have to be so darned perfect?

Since she had figured his sister would probably be riding with them, she was surprised to see the car was empty.

"Vanessa's meeting us there," he said to her unasked question.

"Oh, okay. Where are we going?" He sure looked good. Today he wore dark gray slacks, an open-necked white shirt and a black leather jacket. Joanna had dressed carefully, too—and as conservatively as her wardrobe would permit. She'd put on a short black knit dress, black tights and her black suede boots. And she'd slung the red shawl her mother had made her around her shoulders. But she hadn't toned down her makeup or her hair. She wasn't trying to impress anybody. It was her work that counted, not the way she looked or dressed.

"Canlis," he said in answer to her question. "It's one of my favorite restaurants."

"Mine, too." Not that Joanna frequented the legendary restaurant often. But, like most longtime Seattle residents, she loved its ambience and gorgeous view of Lake Union. And the food was to die for. It also had the bonus of being quiet enough to actually talk to your dinner companions, unlike a lot of the new places where noise seemed to be part of the decor.

"That's a beautiful shawl," he said, giving her a sidelong glance before swinging out into traffic.

"Thank you. My mother made it."

"I thought maybe you did."

She was ridiculously pleased that he'd remembered the crocheted dress in her portfolio and that she'd told him she did her own crocheting and knitting. "No, she was the one who taught me to crochet and knit. It's probably one of the reasons I first became interested in fashion."

"You owe her, then." He shifted gears, and accelerated.

"I do. She's great." She could see his assistant was right. He liked to drive. Fast. Then again, anyone owning a car like this one would definitely like speed. "What kind of car is this, anyway?" she asked after he shifted gears again.

"It's a Ferrari."

"It's beautiful." Joanna wondered what her dad would say if he could see it. He thought all things Italian were better than anything anyone else could produce.

"Thank you. I admit it. I love cars. I have a more sensible one, too, but I prefer to drive this one."

For a while, they didn't talk as he expertly navigated the traffic and she covertly studied him. He had nice hands, she decided, with long fingers and well-groomed nails. They rested almost lovingly on the steering wheel, which made her imagine they would rest just as lovingly on a woman's skin. The unbidden thought caused her to squirm a bit. *Can't you at least try to keep your imagination out of the R-rated zone? You know he's off-limits, so cut out the inappropriate thoughts.*

Even as she lectured herself, she couldn't help wondering why Marcus wasn't married. She knew he was thirty-five, soon to be thirty-six; she'd done a search on him. She also knew a lot about his background because she'd read all the articles her search had turned up. A man as wealthy, successful and sexy as he was had to be considered a catch. It wasn't as if he hadn't done his share of dating. In fact, a couple of the stories she'd read about him came from the society pages of the local newspaper, and according to them he had only recently ended a relationship with one Amanda Warren—herself a prominent member of Who's Who in Seattle. She was one of the beautiful people, too. One photo taken when the two of them had attended a charity dinner showed a tall, elegant blonde with a dazzling smile.

Boy, if Joanna had been in the Warren woman's shoes, she would have held on to Marcus any way she could. Not that she ever *would* be in those shoes, but a girl could dream, couldn't she?

Of course, having a relationship with Marcus wouldn't

all be roses. She wouldn't be crazy about attending tons of charity dinners and doing all that society stuff, but even though she was different and wanted different things than the Warren woman probably wanted, dating Marcus Barlow—at least for a while—wouldn't be a hardship. He probably thought nothing of whisking a date off to Paris for the weekend. If only she was the kind of person who wanted a fling. *You're not, though. You have serious goals and you want the kind of marriage Georgie has. Remember that.* Yeah, Joanna thought wryly, she wanted it all, and she wanted it all her own way.

"You're awfully quiet," he said, startling her.

"Oh, sorry. I was lost in my thoughts." She knew her face had heated. If he'd known she was fantasizing about him, what would he think?

"Take a penny for them?"

She laughed. "They're hardly worth it. I was just thinking…about my boss," she fibbed. "And how he'd better get on the stick and hire someone to replace me." That wasn't really a lie. She *had* been thinking just that earlier.

"He hasn't done that yet?"

"No. He's barely even interviewed. The problem is, he travels too much. Doesn't leave much time for mundane things like finding a new assistant."

"I think I already told you I'd be in serious trouble if my assistant left. She's like my right hand. Cut it off, I couldn't function."

"I offered to do the interviewing for him, but he blew me off. I don't think he trusts me."

"And how long did you say you'd worked for him?"

"Six years, going on seven."

"During which I imagine you've run the office not only while he travels, but probably most of the time even when he's there."

"Yes."

"And he trusts you to do that."

"Yes."

"Then he's an idiot for not letting you find a replacement. And frankly, if that's his attitude, I wouldn't worry about him."

"Oh, believe me, I'm not." She wondered what Marcus would think if she told him how she *really* felt about Chick. Of course, if he knew how stupid she'd been to get mixed up with her boss on a personal level, he'd probably lose all respect for her.

Before she had time to explore *that* sobering thought, Marcus had swung into the front entrance of the restaurant and handed the valet parking attendant his keys.

Joanna enjoyed the way the valet—who knew Marcus by name—acted toward him, and then the maitre d'— who couldn't have been more attentive and who personally escorted them to a choice table in a corner by the windows. As it was a beautiful, sunny day, the water of Lake Union shimmered as if sprinkled with hundreds of tiny jewels.

"Vanessa should be here soon," Marcus said as they were seated. "She had a class this morning and was coming here afterward."

"Where does she go to school?"

"She's taking some courses at the Art Institute." Then he added, "She dropped out of college after the spring semester."

Joanna could tell he wasn't pleased by this. "Maybe design school would be a better choice for her?"

He shrugged. "She said she needs a break from college. I hope she goes back. I'd like to see her get a fine arts degree. At least then, if designing jewelry doesn't work out for her, she could go on, get her master's and possibly teach."

Joanna wondered if Marcus and her mother had compared notes. He certainly sounded like her mother, who'd wanted the same thing for Joanna. "Teaching isn't for everyone, either," she said gently.

"I know that, but it would be a great fallback for her. At least until she marries."

Joanna would have liked to say something else, but just then their waiter approached, poured glasses of water for them and gave Marcus the wine list. While Marcus was studying it, a tall young woman walked in their direction, and Marcus looked up, smiling. "Here she is." He stood, kissed his sister's cheek and turned to Joanna. "Joanna, this is my sister, Vanessa. Vanessa, Joanna Spinelli."

Vanessa was gorgeous, Joanna thought. Very tall, probably five-ten. In her heeled boots, she was pretty much eye to eye with her brother. Thin and svelte, she had thick wheat-blond hair that fell in shining waves and striking blue eyes fringed with long lashes. She wore low-cut faded jeans, formfitting layered T-shirts, one white, one dark blue, a wide brown leather belt and a lot of chunky silver jewelry—probably her own designs. Joanna wondered what Marcus thought of his sister's outfit. It wasn't exactly Junior League.

"Hi," Vanessa said, giving Joanna a cautious smile. "It's nice to meet you."

"Thank you. It's very nice to meet you, too." Joanna had the distinct feeling Vanessa Barlow hadn't been thrilled about this meeting, which meant she probably was less than enthusiastic about combining their design talents into one show. Joanna just hoped her opinion didn't sway Marcus, and that he would stick to their agreement. Because if he wasn't one hundred percent on board with it, Joanna knew he could easily get out of the contract.

In the bustle of Vanessa getting seated and Marcus consulting them about possible wine selections— Joanna declined, knowing she needed her wits about her today—she had a chance to really study Vanessa. The girl was certainly a looker, stunning even, with her high cheekbones, elegant turned-up nose and large eyes. And she had that confident way of carrying herself that reminded Joanna of the models she had used for the photos in her portfolio. In fact, wouldn't Vanessa be the perfect model for the black satin skinny pants and ivory lace halter top Joanna was currently working on? The ensemble would be one of four in her collection geared toward the young end of the market. The idea excited Joanna, and she couldn't help smiling at Vanessa.

"I love your jewelry designs," she said once Vanessa was settled and had had a chance to look over the menu.

"Thank you."

Joanna didn't miss the fact that Vanessa hadn't commented on her clothing designs. Had she seen any of them? Joanna only had six designs on her website, but those six were ones she was proudest of. She was about to ask her about them when their waiter reappeared with the wine Marcus had ordered, as well as iced tea for Joanna.

Once the wine was poured, they placed their orders, and after the waiter had finally left them alone again, Joanna turned to Vanessa and said, "What do you think of your brother's idea that we should combine our shows?"

Vanessa shrugged. "Honestly? I'm not sure. I mean, your designs are beautiful. I did look at your website. But they're so different from what I do. Your clothing is romantic and classical, geared to a different kind of woman than I design for." She took a deep breath, and met Joanna's gaze squarely. "You may not agree but my designs are meant for a younger, more cutting-edge market."

Joanna nodded. She liked Vanessa's honesty. "I do agree that on the surface our two sensibilities don't seem to mesh, but after thinking about it and playing with the possibilities, I think combining the two could work very well. You wouldn't know this, because I don't have any examples on my website, but I'm going to have at least four pieces in the collection that are strictly for the youth market." She smiled. "In fact, the moment I saw you, I thought how perfect you'd be to model one of the outfits." Her smile widened as she saw the look on Vanessa's face. "And your jewelry would look fantastic with the outfit I have in mind."

"Me? Model?" Vanessa said. Her gaze moved to Marcus.

Joanna looked at Marcus, too. He was frowning.

"No," he said.

No? Just like that? Joanna opened her mouth to say something, but before she could, Vanessa said, "Excuse me?"

"You heard me," he said. "I don't want you modeling."

If her brother Tony had ever talked to her in that tone of voice, Joanna knew she would probably have done whatever it was he'd forbidden her to do just out of spite. She looked at Vanessa.

Vanessa turned to her and smiled. "You know what? I would love to see what you're doing for the youth market. And despite what my brother says, if I decide I'd like to model for you, I will."

Joanna didn't dare look at Marcus. She wasn't afraid of what she'd see on his face; she was afraid of what he might see on *hers.* She wanted to cheer. Good for Vanessa. She might be young, and Marcus might be a father figure for her, but she had guts. Joanna decided then and there that no matter what, she wanted to work with Vanessa—for the show and just possibly for the future, too.

"In fact," Vanessa continued, "why don't I drive you home today instead of Marcus? That way, I can see your work and make my decision quickly."

Now Joanna did glance at Marcus. And she could see, even though he tried to disguise it, that he was furious. Suddenly she felt bad. She liked him. In fact, she more than liked him. And he was giving her this huge opportunity. Did she *really* want to take a chance on blowing it?

Turning back to Vanessa, she said, "Maybe it would be better if you and your brother talked this over in private first."

"That's not necessary," Marcus said, cutting in. "In fact, it's probably a good idea for Vanessa to see your designs in person. That way we can at least get one thing settled today." His words left no doubt that he would deal with the *other thing* later.

Joanna hoped his anger, still so apparent, didn't spill over to include her. Even the thought caused her heart to beat faster. Turning to him again, she gave him a warm smile. "Thank you. I'll be glad to have the decision about combining our shows settled today, too." She hoped her eyes would convey the fact that she sympathized with him and wasn't taking sides. She also hoped he knew she was sorry she'd ever brought up the idea of Vanessa modeling. If she didn't think it would just cause more trouble, she'd even say so.

"Yes," Vanessa chimed in, her voice as sweet as syrup, "thank you, Marcus. I'm glad you've finally decided to join the twenty-first century."

Joanna swallowed. She wished she could just quietly disappear and let the siblings duke it out. There was obviously a lot more going on here than appeared on the surface. And, if she wasn't extremely careful, both now and in the future, she could very easily get caught in the cross fire.

Chapter Seven

Marcus seethed all the way back to the office. He was no longer simply angry over the whole modeling idea—he had no doubt at all that Vanessa would agree to do it—now he was almost more upset about the way she'd talked to him. *Enter the twenty-first century!* How dare she say something like that, and in front of Joanna, of all people?

It was then, when Vanessa had so disdainfully dismissed his ideas as dated and old-fashioned, that he'd realized how much he cared what Joanna thought. The realization had stunned him. Up until that moment he'd simply thought his undeniable attraction to her was more physical than anything else, so it would be fairly easy to ignore it. But he couldn't fool himself into thinking that way any longer. The truth was, he had wanted to kiss her that day in the storeroom, would have kissed her if Brenda hadn't interrupted them, and now he wanted her respect and admiration, not just a sexual awareness. That kind of attraction didn't necessarily last. Respect and admiration did.

And he wanted it to last.

The thought was sobering.

When had he changed from thinking Joanna was an impossible choice for him, on any personal level, to thinking he wanted to explore the possibility of her becoming a part of his life? She would have to change some things about herself, of course, but that was easily accomplished. He knew he had the ability to convince others of his opinions; he did it every day. Maybe not Vanessa—at least lately—but surely if he and Joanna became involved, she was mature enough to understand she would need to change to fit into his world.

He wondered what Joanna had been thinking when Vanessa said what she did at lunch. For a moment there, he'd gotten the idea Joanna was sorry she'd brought up the whole subject of modeling, but maybe that was just wishful thinking on his part.

Damn Vanessa. He'd have a thing or two to say to her when he got home tonight. He would *not* be undermined in such a public way again. He still couldn't believe she'd done it. Especially after she'd apologized to him for her recent bad behavior. So much for words. From now on, it would be actions that counted.

By the time he reached his office, he'd only managed to make himself more upset and he knew he had better put the entire episode out of his mind, at least for the remainder of the afternoon. He had too much work to do to have his brain occupied with anything other than business. And because he was extremely self-disciplined once he made a decision, he managed to do just that.

But the moment he arrived home that evening and saw Vanessa's little Fiat sitting in the garage, all his anger with her flooded back.

Intent on confronting her before he did anything else, he entered the house. He found his sister in the living room, curled up in one of the armchairs and lazily leafing through a magazine. She glanced up when he entered. "Hi," she said, all innocence.

He kept his tone measured. "So tell me. What did you think of Joanna's designs?"

She gave him an impish grin. "You were right. I really like her work, especially the pieces she's doing for the younger market."

"Good. Glad you've decided to cooperate." He took off his jacket and put it and his briefcase on the sofa, then sat on its arm. He said nothing; his silence would be more potent than any mention of the modeling. He knew he wouldn't have long to wait before she couldn't resist bringing up the subject herself.

Just as he'd thought, only a few moments passed before she said, "The outfit she wants me to model is absolutely perfect for me. In fact, I told her I wanted to buy it." Her voice took on a defiant edge as her eyes met his. Only the way she straightened in her chair betrayed an underlying uncertainty.

The only sounds in the room were the hiss and spit of the fire in the fireplace as a log settled and the chimes of the grandfather clock in the foyer as it signaled the hour. Even Cleo, their mother's ten-year-old chocolate Lab, who had walked in a moment earlier, sensed the tension and curled up quietly nearby, her big eyes wary.

"I—I gave her a deposit on it before I left today," Vanessa said in a rush. "It's a beautiful outfit, Marcus."

Marcus was determined to keep his temper under control, so his tone, although firm when he finally answered, was quiet. "Whether it's beautiful or not is totally irrelevant. We'll discuss the actual modeling in a minute. What I want to talk about first is the way you spoke to me at lunch." Vanessa opened her mouth, but he forestalled her by raising his hand. "I'm not finished."

She swallowed.

"Do not ever make fun of me or show such a total lack of respect for me in public again. What you say at home, in private, is one thing, even though I would think you would choose your words more carefully here, too, but embarrassing me in front of someone else, especially someone I'm working with on a professional level, is inexcusable. And I will not stand for it." Now his voice rose in volume. "Do you understand?"

Again she swallowed, then wet her lips. "I—I…"

"Do. You. Understand?" All his pent-up anger…and hurt…and disappointment in her…shuddered in the air. "I…"

She was shaken, he could see that.

She took a deep breath and collected herself, then in a burst of bravado, said, "You know, Marcus, you showed a lack of respect for *me* when you wouldn't even *listen* to what Joanna had to say about the modeling." Two spots of color appeared on Vanessa's cheeks. "I mean, you just said no, like I was some little kid. I'm not a child. I—I think you could have at least said let's talk about it later…or something…" The bravado disappeared, and her voice trailed off. A tear rolled down her cheek.

Marcus didn't want to admit it, but in fairness, her point was valid. He had done the same thing to her that he was accusing her of doing. He sighed. "I apologize for that. You're right. I should have been more diplomatic."

Swiping away the tear, she said, "Thank you. And

I...I apologize for what I said. I was just mad, that's all. I was embarrassed that you'd talked to me that way in front of Joanna. I—I like her."

For the first time that evening, he smiled. "I'm glad we cleared the air."

She nodded. "Me, too. So it's okay for me to model, then?"

"I didn't say that. I still don't think it's a good idea for you to model in the show."

"But, Marcus, can't you see you're being completely unreasonable?"

Marcus sighed again. Why was she so set upon doing this? It wasn't as if she had aspirations of a modeling career. That, he could possibly understand, although he still wouldn't want her doing it. Modeling was not a suitable pursuit for a young woman like Vanessa. He couldn't help feeling she was just saying she wanted to model at the show because he didn't want her to.

She wanted reasonable. He'd give her reasonable. "I don't think you've thought about this from all angles. You'll need to be available to talk to potential customers of your own that night. If you're modeling, you won't be able to give your full attention to your own business."

"Oh, that's ridicu—" She stopped herself, visibly took a breath. More quietly, she said, "Of course I will. It's not like there's going to be a runway show and I'll only be out among the customers for a few minutes. The models will be circulating the entire evening, won't they? And I can accessorize my outfit any way I want to—Joanna said so—so I'll be wearing quite a bit of my own jewelry.

"Come on, Marcus. It'll be fun," Vanessa added in the wheedling tone she always used to soften him up. "I don't know why you're so set against this."

"It's not the image you should be projecting."

Her eyes narrowed. "What are you *talking* about? What're you afraid of? That I might like it and then decide I want to be a model? Is that it?"

"I'm not afraid of anything. I just don't like the idea. It's not suitable." But now that she'd said it, that's exactly what he *was* afraid of. His sister was entirely too impressionable. And even though he liked Joanna—right now she wasn't the best role model for Vanessa.

"I don't understand you. I thought you'd be happy that I have agreed to work with Joanna."

"Working with her by combining your talents is not the same as modeling for her."

"Marcus, you need to lighten up. For someone who's only thirty-five, you act like an old man sometimes. You're not my father."

"How well I know that," he muttered.

Vanessa sighed. "Look, I—I love you. I don't want to hurt you, but you can't control everything in my life. It's not like I want to do drugs or become a groupie with a rock band or give all my money to some worthless jerk. I just want to model in the show. For *one* evening. And you haven't given me a single good reason why I shouldn't. So, I'm sorry, but the only way you can stop me is to cancel the entire show."

Marcus would have liked nothing better than to do just that. But he knew—and she knew it, too—that he wouldn't cancel the show. For one thing, he'd given his word, and he never went back on his word. For another, he didn't really want to cancel. He just wanted to shake some sense into his willful sister.

Where had this stubborn streak of hers come from?

It was on days like this that Marcus wished he had someone he could talk to. A best friend or a brother he could count on. Even a sensible mother who would dispense practical advice. But there was no one. His college friends had long ago gone their own ways. Most of them led distinctly different lives from his.

"What in the world is all this ruckus about?"

Both Marcus and Vanessa turned at the sound of their mother's voice. Laurette, frowning, stood in the doorway of the living room. As always, she looked impeccable in a beautiful gray wool dress and her pearls.

"I could hear you all the way up in my bedroom," she said. "I'm surprised the neighbors haven't complained."

"Just a disagreement, that's all," Marcus said, standing. He walked over and kissed her cheek. "I'm sorry we disturbed you."

"Disagreement about what?"

Marcus knew there was no point in getting his mother in the middle of this. "It's not important."

"If it's not important, I can't see why you two are making such a fuss."

Marcus looked over at Vanessa. She shrugged as if to say this was his problem, not hers. "Excuse me, but I need to make a phone call," she said. Then, sweetly, "Thank you for the lovely lunch today, Marcus."

When she'd left the room, Laurette said, "Are you going to tell me what this is about or not, Marcus?" She sat in the chair Vanessa had vacated and Cleo, tail wagging, got up and nuzzled her leg. Absently, Laurette scratched behind the dog's ears.

"It's nothing, really." Marcus reached for his briefcase and jacket.

"Honestly, Marcus, sometimes you two drive me crazy."

Marcus almost laughed. They drove *her* crazy? Every single person in his family drove *him* crazy. Some days he was sure he'd lose his mind. "Where's Tad today?" he said, to change the subject.

"He had an interview this afternoon." Laurette smiled, obviously pleased to be able to relay positive news to Marcus.

"Oh? Where?"

"I believe he was going to that new tech company. The one that just opened on Rydell Road."

At least Tad was making an effort. "Good."

"Yes, he was very pleased to have gotten the interview. All on his own, too."

This last, Marcus knew, was a dig at him, even though his mother knew full well why he refused to set up any more interviews for Tad after the last fiasco. If Tad found a job, it would have to be through his own efforts. "I hope it went well. Is he going to be here for dinner?"

She looked at her watch. "I believe so."

Saying he would see her at dinner, too, he also excused himself and headed to the other wing and his own quarters. He changed his clothes, fixed himself a drink and turned on the news. But he couldn't relax or concentrate. He couldn't get the argument with Vanessa, and the meeting with Joanna that had provoked it, out of his mind.

After mulling everything over again, he decided he wanted to see this outfit Vanessa would be modeling. He guessed, if it was as beautiful as the designs he'd already seen, maybe it wouldn't be so bad to have Vanessa modeling it this one time.

In addition, he wanted to see all the designs Joanna had ready for the show, as well as the ones she was still working on. Maybe she had exaggerated her progress. Not that he thought she had, but still, he needed to be sure.

He would call her.

In fact, he would call her right now.

He ignored the little voice in the back of his mind that said he had wanted a reason to call her and this one was perfect.

Reaching for his cell, he scrolled through his contacts and found Joanna's number. She sounded a bit breathless when she answered.

"Did I get you at a bad time?" he asked.

"No, no, not at all. I'm just coming back from getting the mail. Hold on a minute. Let me unlock the door." A few minutes later she said, "Okay, I'm back in my place now."

"I won't keep you long. I just finished talking to Vanessa and she says she was very impressed with your work. That's what prompted this call, in fact. I'd like to see what you've got ready for the show, too."

"Oh, yes, of course. All you've seen are photos. Um, when would you like to come?"

"I was thinking about tomorrow."

"I'm sorry, but I have to work tomorrow."

"What about tomorrow evening? Unless you have plans?"

"Um, no, no plans. Okay, tomorrow would be fine. What time do you want to come?"

"What time is good for you?"

"Six o'clock?"

"That's perfect. I'll head over straight from my office."

"All right. I'll tell the security guard to expect you. Um, the best place to park is around the corner. There's a garage."

"Okay, thanks. And, Joanna…"

"Yes?"

"Since I'll be interrupting the dinner hour, it's only fair that I feed you afterward."

"You don't have to do that."

"I know I don't have to, but I'd like to."

"Well, if you put it that way…that would be nice. There are some good places within walking distance. Do you like Italian?"

"One of my favorites."

He was smiling as he disconnected the call.

On Friday morning, when Joanna arrived at the office, Chick was already there. She did a double take. Chick never showed up at the office before her. He was a notorious night owl and hardly ever crawled out of bed before nine.

He ostentatiously looked at his watch. Joanna bit back a smile. She wasn't late. In fact, she was early. It was only seven-fifty. Too bad, she thought. She knew he was still royally ticked off about her quitting and would have enjoyed any reason to find fault with her work.

"My, my," she said. "This is a red-letter day. You haven't shown up this early in years."

Ignoring that, Chick said, "I have someone coming in at eight-fifteen for an interview."

"Oh?" The agency they were using hadn't notified Joanna.

"The agency called yesterday while you were *off.*" Chick said the word *off* as if Joanna should have been at work instead.

Joanna decided she would get on with her morning. If Chick wanted to elaborate, he would. If not, who cared? She only had one more week to work. After that, it didn't matter to her what he did or who he did it with. For that matter, she didn't care who he hired, either. Good luck to him finding someone who would work as hard as she had over the past years.

But he seemed determined to tell her about the interviewee whether she wanted to hear about her or not, and he followed Joanna around as she prepared the office for the morning.

"According to the agency, this girl will be available to start on Monday. If I like her, of course."

"Of course." Joanna cleaned up the little kitchen—he never left it clean after her day off—which irritated her, yet what could she do about it? She was glad to see the new supply of individual coffee servings had come yesterday while she was gone. They had just about been out and she wasn't sure if the order would make it on time.

"I'm going to need you to work all five days next week," he said.

Joanna sighed. She'd been expecting this. "Fine, as long as I get paid overtime for the extra day."

"Look, I gave you Thursdays off out of the goodness of my heart. The least you can do after leaving me in the lurch like this is work this one last Thursday."

"You didn't give me anything. We agreed, up front, that I would take less money if I could have a four-day workweek." She could have added that she'd done more work in her four days than most people would have been able to accomplish in five or six, but why waste her breath?

"Fine," he mimicked, "I'll pay you the extra." Turning away, he added, "I'll need you to stay late tonight, too."

"Sorry. I can't. I have plans for tonight."

"You'll have to cancel them."

Okay. She'd been reasonable about everything else, but enough was enough. "Excuse me? I don't *have* to do anything. I've agreed to work an extra day next week, but that's as far as I'm going."

"If you want a letter of reference from me, you'll do what I need you to do. The invoices need to go in the mail today, remember?"

"Number one, I don't need a letter of reference from you. Number two, when have I ever not gotten the invoices out on time?"

"There's always a first time," he said, glaring at her before turning away and heading toward his office.

"Oh, go suck an egg," she mumbled under her breath.

"What did you say?" he demanded, swinging around.

Joanna had had a bellyful by now and for two cents she'd stop what she was doing, clean out her desk, grab her purse and jacket and good luck to him. But no matter what else she might be, she was her mother's daughter, and her mother was the one who'd taught her you never burn your bridges. Besides, Chick owed her a week's vacation pay, which she fully expected to receive along with her last paycheck, and if she walked out on him, she'd never see the money unless she sued him. So Joanna tamped down her indignation and resentment and met Chick's angry gaze levelly. "I just said I'd better suck it up and get legs."

He stared at her for a long moment, then stalked into his office and slammed the door.

Joanna put her head in her hands. One more week, she thought. Just one. She could stand anything for a week. Hopefully this woman coming in today would work out and Chick would hire her. Because Joanna couldn't imagine how miserable next week would be if he *hadn't* found someone by the time her notice was over and he was forced to use a temp. Oh, God, it didn't bear thinking about.

Well, she'd better do all she could to make sure that didn't happen, which meant getting every last bit of work done so Chick would have nothing to complain about. But it was going to be a horrendous day. Because in addition to making sure all the invoices went out, she had several errant customer orders to track—no easy task—as well as half a dozen new orders to process. Since the new orders would take the least amount of time, she would get those out of the way first.

She was working on the first of the new orders when the outer door opened, and a tall, curvy redhead walked in. Joanna took one look at her and knew if she had even a modicum of expertise, Chick would hire her. She was too gorgeous for him to pass up. Thirty-six

C, Joanna figured, looking at her formfitting taupe sweater. Oh, no, Chick wouldn't let this girl go.

"Hi," the girl said. "I'm Lonnie McKee. I have an appointment with Mr. Newton." There was a quaver in her voice.

Joanna smiled at the girl. She wanted to say, *Don't be nervous, you've got this job in the bag.* "I'll tell him you're here," she said instead. She pressed the intercom button and announced the girl's arrival.

"Send her in," Chick said curtly.

Still mad, Joanna thought. What an ass he was. And what an idiot *she* was for ever falling for his line.

The interview didn't even last twenty minutes. Joanna had only processed two of the new orders when Chick's office door opened again and the McKee girl, followed by a smugly smiling Chick, exited his office. Lonnie McKee's hazel eyes were bright.

"Joanna," he said, "Miss McKee will be starting work here on Monday, but she's also agreed to stay for an hour or two today so you can orient her and tell her what to expect."

Joanna's heart sank. Her busy day had just gotten impossible. She would have to practically kill herself to get everything done so that she could leave on time. But she didn't hesitate, just smiled and nodded and said, "Okay. Come and sit down, Miss McKee."

"Oh, please call me Lonnie."

"All right, Lonnie."

For the next thirty minutes, Joanna gave Lonnie as many pointers as she could. She wanted to be honest, to warn Lonnie of the many pitfalls of working for Chick, but she didn't want to frighten her away. And Joanna had a feeling she *could* be frightened away, because even though Lonnie had seemed sophisticated when she first walked in, within a few minutes of talking to her, Joanna could see she wasn't. In fact, Lonnie seemed naive.

She wondered how long it would take Chick to get this girl into his bed. Poor thing, Joanna felt sorry for her already. But Lonnie's future wasn't Joanna's problem, was it? Her own future was what was at stake here. Lonnie could worry about herself.

"You might need to work some overtime," she told Lonnie. "Will that be a problem?"

Lonnie shook her head. "No. Actually, Mr. Newton mentioned that it might be necessary, and I told him I had no problem with it." She smiled at Joanna. "I'm single and I still live at home. I don't have a lot of responsibilities."

"That's good." Joanna was having a hard time thinking of Chick as Mr. Newton.

"I plan to try to find my own place fairly quickly, though," Lonnie added. "Um, why are you leaving, if you don't mind my asking?"

"I have an opportunity to do what I've always wanted to do—something I've worked toward for years." Joanna glanced at Chick's closed door. She knew he wouldn't be thrilled if he heard her talking about anything personal. "I'm a fashion designer and I'm going to do that full-time."

"Oh, that's wonderful!" Lonnie said. "I'm envious. I have no creative talent at all."

"Thank you. I'm excited. I admit it."

"I don't blame you. I'm glad, though, that you'll be here next week to train me."

"Yes. I didn't have anyone to train me. I had to figure everything out on my own."

"Um…" Lonnie lowered her voice and glanced at Chick's closed door. "Is, um, Mr. Newton nice to work for?"

"Well," Joanna said, mentally crossing her fingers, "he can be tough, like any boss. I mean, he wants things done right. But he's not an ogre or anything. And he's fair."

This was true. Chick *was* fair about work. In fact, he had been a good boss until Joanna became personally involved with him. If she'd had sense enough to keep their relationship one that was strictly business, she wouldn't have had any problems here. For a moment, she almost considered warning Lonnie, but wisely discarded the impulse. Lonnie would have to learn her own lessons.

Keep your eye on the goal line. Remember what you've been working toward all these years. And it's almost here.

Joanna managed to cover everything she needed to in less than an hour. Lonnie left soon after, thanking her profusely and saying she'd be there promptly at eight Monday morning.

After that, Joanna worked like a whirlwind. In a way, it was a good thing she was so busy because otherwise she'd have been unable to do anything but watch the clock and obsess over the coming evening.

Yet she couldn't entirely stop herself from thinking about it. And whenever she did, her stomach would flutter. About the dozenth time this happened, she lectured herself sternly.

Tonight is not a date.

Quit acting like a giddy teenager.

Marcus is coming to see your designs, not you.

And yet he *had* invited her to dinner. *Just because he's thoughtful and nice, that's all. Not because he's interested in you.*

But no matter how many times she told herself this, she knew it wasn't quite true. Oh, he was thoughtful and nice. That part was true. But the sexual tension between them wasn't her imagination. He was as attracted to her as she was to him.

She should have said no to dinner. That would have been the smart thing to do. She should keep any time spent with him strictly business. Because nothing had changed since the last time she'd thought about this. Marcus Barlow was still way out of her league. He would never be interested in any kind of permanent relationship with someone like her. And Joanna wasn't interested in anything else, not at this point in her life. She'd learned her lesson well with Chick. She wanted what Georgie had: a Prince Charming, a wedding ring and a family.

Anything less was out of the question.

Chapter Eight

Although she had wanted to make some phone calls to her *own* suppliers—in particular to a new fabric store she'd discovered online—Joanna instead worked through her lunch hour, eating her chicken sandwich at her desk. Better that than taking a chance on not getting office jobs finished by the time she needed to leave. She only stopped working to answer a text from Georgie and an email from her mother. Other than that, she barely took time for potty breaks.

And thank the Lord, Chick left for an appointment at two. Knowing he had to drive out to Sandpoint, Joanna figured he couldn't possibly get back to the office before their four o'clock Friday closing time—not that she thought he would. Especially as she was almost finished with the invoices before he left. He couldn't resist lobbing one veiled threat, though, saying he would check in with her later to make sure there were no emergencies.

She rolled her eyes once the door closed behind him. *Later.* In other words, near the end of the day. Probably five minutes before quitting time. To make sure she didn't skip out early.

How childish he was. Did all men at some point feel the need to roar and bare their teeth to prove their

manliness or something? The thought reminded her
how Marcus had tried to intimidate his sister over the
modeling suggestion Joanna had made. Although he
hadn't threatened Vanessa, he'd certainly tried to im-
pose his will.

Maybe all men *did* feel the need to control the
women in their lives. The thought was unsettling, because Joanna had decided at an early age that no one,
and certainly no *man,* would ever tell her what to do,
especially as it pertained to her private life…and her
choices. She'd witnessed enough of that with her father—who, even though he was a really nice man and
obviously loved her mother—still wanted to be in
charge. Of everything.

And her brother Tony! How Sharon put up with his
manipulation, Joanna didn't know. It was one thing to
be under the thumb of a boss in a working situation. Everyone had to compromise certain stances at times; it
was called being practical and realistic. Deciding what
was important to you and what you could sacrifice to
achieve your longer-term goals spelled *m-a-t-u-r-i-t-y.*

But on a personal level?

That was a different story. She couldn't imagine allowing some man to tell her how to live her life: what
to wear, what to eat, what to read, what politics or reli-
gion or way of life to believe in. Actually, she couldn't
imagine *anyone* controlling what she thought and did.

Not even Marcus Barlow?

Not even him.

When she was too young to know any better, she'd
imagined that only Italian men like her father had that
seemingly built-in need to be the center of the universe
by bending the women they loved to their will. She'd

attributed their behavior to the pampering and adoration they received from their mothers.

As much as she loved her granny Carmela, Joanna wasn't blind to the fact that Granny Carmela thought her oldest child and only son could do no wrong. Nor could he do "a woman's work."

By college age, though, Joanna had realized other cultures also relegated their women to a much lower tier than their men. In fact, *most* did. But she had still believed Prince Charmings existed. Shoot, if she were completely honest with herself, down deep, she *still* did. At least she *wanted* to.

But maybe she'd been wrong to cling to this fantasy. Maybe the reason she still didn't have her so-called Prince Charming and everything that went along with him was that Prince Charmings didn't exist and she'd been unwilling to settle for less.

She sighed. Not everyone settled. Georgie hadn't. Had she? Was Zach Prince, Georgie's husband, really and truly as marvelous as Georgie made him out to be? How could anyone know the truth about a relationship unless they were part of it?

On and on Joanna's thoughts went, getting more and more depressing and confusing, and the excitement she had initially felt over the upcoming visit— *not a date!*—from Marcus, faded a bit. Yet by the time she walked out the door a few minutes after four—and she'd been right, Chick had called to check on her at 3:55!— the butterflies were back, and she couldn't wait to get home. Despite every reason she knew Marcus was wrong for her, she couldn't tamp down the growing feeling that she was teetering on the edge of something unknown, something scary and exciting and amazing.

Something she might not be able to resist, even though she was probably setting herself up for a huge disappointment…or worse.

Luck was with Joanna and the traffic going home wasn't as bad as it could sometimes be. She even reached her parking garage early. It was barely 4:35 when she walked into her apartment.

As she raced around preparing for Marcus's arrival, her qualms took a backseat to her anticipation and growing excitement. By the time her doorbell rang a few minutes after six, her heart was skittering right along with her stomach. Taking several deep breaths and telling herself to calm down—*this is business!*—she slowly walked to the door.

Today Marcus was dressed like the professional CEO he was in a dark suit, light bluish-gray shirt and matching silk tie. She couldn't help noticing the shirt and tie were the exact shade of his spellbinding eyes.

"Right on time," she said, smiling.

His answering smile did nothing to settle her nerves…or the rest of her body. Why did he have to be so darned sexy? And why did her heart have to betray her like this? Said traitorous organ was beating so hard, she was afraid he might be able to hear it. So much for telling herself tonight was only business, she thought wryly. Her brain might actually pretend to believe it, but the rest of her body was more honest.

"C'mon in," she said, grateful she'd managed to sound so normal when she felt anything but. "I apologize for the clutter. Tomorrow my mom and I are looking at several places for me to relocate. Once I do that, I'll have a lot more room to work."

As she explained, she gestured toward the myriad items filling the room: the dress forms, the sewing machine, the large worktable covered with the materials she was currently using, her MacBook, the ironing board and iron set up in the corner, the built-in shelves crammed with supplies and the finished designs hanging on a luggage trolley she'd purchased from a hotel equipment supplier.

Wondering what he thought, she watched as Marcus slowly looked around the room. The memory of Chick's casual disinterest in her design aspirations the one and only time he'd been there was a painful reminder of her past bad judgment. But in this, she knew Marcus *was* different. He'd once been an aspiring artist with his own dreams.

"Was this intended to be a living room?" he asked, now studying her large bulletin board crammed with notes, newspaper articles, reminders of all kinds and dozens of photos. Despite Pinterest—which often gave her ideas—Joanna was a tactile person, and she liked to be able to touch the physical evidence of her passion.

"Yes, which is another reason I need more space." She'd turned her bedroom into a combination bedroom/ living room. In fact, she didn't even have a proper bed. She slept on her sofa. But he didn't have to know that. *This is business.* Maybe if she told herself this enough times it might actually turn out to be true. Did she really *want* it to be true?

Marcus had moved to her worktable and was looking down at the pattern pieces she'd pinned and cut out last night. The work-in-progress emulated something Sue Wong—a designer Joanna admired—had said in an interview. It walked "a fine line between art and commerce" and was geared to Joanna's dreamed-of customer: a young woman who was spirited, smart, independent-thinking, yet classical and romantic and elegant. Georgie, actually. Joanna smiled.

Marcus glanced up, catching the smile. He gave her a quizzical look.

"I was just thinking about my best friend, who inspired that design," Joanna explained.

"What's it going to be?" Marcus asked, picking up and examining a bit of the leftover jersey matte fabric that wasn't pinned to the pattern.

"Evening pants and jacket."

He nodded. "I didn't think you'd use something like this for a daytime outfit. Then again…" He chuckled. "What do I know?"

Obviously, he knew a lot, whether he realized it or not. After all, he attended all kinds of charity dinners, balls, concerts, even the opera, because Joanna had seen a mention of his attendance recently at McCaw Hall. He had to have absorbed some fashion sense with all that exposure. But he was wrong about the daytime remark, because the jersey matte was sturdy, draped well, was more durable than it looked and could work beautifully for a certain type of dress or daytime occasion.

Joanna let him continue to browse around on his own. She was enjoying watching him and the thoughtful way he inspected her workplace and was in no hurry to steer him to the finished pieces she intended for the show. He had now walked back to the bulletin board and was studying an article about Sarah Burton, who had taken over the house of Alexander McQueen when the famed designer had died.

"She's a designer I admire tremendously," Joanna said, walking over and joining him. "She's the one who designed the Duchess of Cambridge's wedding dress." Chick would have asked who the hell the Duchess of Cambridge was. The fact that Marcus hadn't vividly underscored how different the two men were.

"And she?" He pointed to a photo of Stella McCartney.

"I love her work, too. She created a line that's wearable and appealing, according to the critics. Do you know who she is?"

He met her gaze. "Paul McCartney's daughter?"

Why, his eyes were actually twinkling! Joanna grinned. "So your sister was wrong. You *have* joined the twenty-first century."

When he laughed, Joanna finally began to relax. The man might be a lot of things and he might not be the man for her, but he had a sense of humor and he didn't mind being teased. Any man who could laugh at himself was all right. More than all right. He might even turn out to be a Prince Charming after all. For someone, anyway.

After a few more minutes, he walked toward the finished designs. "Are these the ones you have ready for the show?"

"Yes, I think so, although I reserve the right to change my mind. Um, why don't you sit in that chair?" She gestured to a white wicker chair she sometimes collapsed in to think. "And I'll show you the garments as if you were a customer in a high-class salon."

The first designs she brought over for him to see were the ones he'd already seen in photographs. There were six in all.

"They look even better than they did in the photographs," he said.

Next she showed him the green velvet one-shoulder gown she'd adapted for Georgie and her pregnancy, even though it would not be a part of the show because Georgie wanted to wear it before then. "My best friend is pregnant," she explained. "And she commissioned this for the holidays."

He nodded thoughtfully. "Are you planning to do maternity clothes?"

"I hadn't been. But while I was working on this piece for Georgie, I did think it might be fun to eventually do some designs for pregnant women who want a couture look." She shrugged. "I don't know, I'm just toying with that idea. Right now my entire focus is on the upcoming show."

Next she showed him the most tailored piece in her collection—a gray moire skirt and jacket with a narrow silver belt and white satin pleated shell that would be worn under the jacket. "I see a woman wearing this for afternoon tea in a nice hotel, or some women might even wear it to work, depending on what kind of work they do," she explained.

"I like that a lot," he said.

There were two others remaining: a cocktail dress in a shimmery gold charmeuse and a softly flowered chiffon at-home outfit with wide pants and a snug, flocked, cap-sleeved top.

The last outfit she brought out was the one Vanessa would model: black satin tapered pants that would be altered to fit Vanessa like a second skin, paired with an ivory lace halter top lined in sheer ivory silk.

"That's the outfit Vanessa wants to model?" he said.

For the first time since he'd arrived, he didn't look or sound pleased.

"Yes. Don't you like it?"

"It's not that I don't like it. I just think it's a bit... revealing...don't you?"

Joanna sighed inwardly. Oh, Lord. He was going to go all conservative and protective of his sister. There wasn't a thing wrong with the pants and top. It was sexy, yes, but in a young, completely acceptable way. Good grief. He was a sophisticated man. Surely he saw the way young women dressed nowadays. The only thing this outfit would reveal of Vanessa was something that couldn't be hidden anyway—the fact she had a terrific figure and was a beautiful, sexy young woman.

"If you're worried about the halter top," she said, "it's fully lined."

"Let me see that," he said, reaching for it.

Joanna handed the garment to him, and when she did, their hands brushed, and she felt a jolt of something very like electricity. It seemed like an omen. Or a warning: Danger Ahead. Had he felt it, too? He must have, yet he said nothing, just took the top.

When he said nothing, just kept looking at it, she said, "I know you still don't want her to do this. I'm really sorry I initiated this problem with you and Vanessa, but I had no idea you'd be against her modeling in the show."

"I know. And she even wants to buy the outfit. I know that, too." Joanna wasn't sure what to say, so she said nothing.

"It's okay. I'm not mad at you." His smile was rueful. "None of this is your fault. My sister is stubborn and seems to delight in doing the exact opposite of anything I might want."

"You're not alone. I think all twenty-year-olds are the same. I used to give my father fits at that age." She laughed. "At times, I still do."

"But as my sister has pointed out more than once, I'm *not* her father, and I won't even be her legal guardian after her twenty-first birthday."

"Does that worry you?"

"A little."

Joanna knew, from reading about him, that his mother was alive. Yet he was Vanessa's guardian? That was interesting. She wondered what was behind *that* story. "I realize I don't know Vanessa very well," she said carefully, "but from what I've seen of her, she seems to have a pretty level head."

"I'm not so sure anymore." He seemed about to say something else but didn't. Instead, he frowned.

"My mother always says it's best to allow people to make their own mistakes because it's the only way they learn." Joanna grimaced. "But when it comes to his children, my father doesn't agree."

"That doesn't seem to work with my family," he said, rising and avoiding her eyes.

Now, why had she said that? She wished she could take the unasked-for advice back. Joanna wanted to kick herself. She'd stepped over the line, and now he was probably wondering how he could get out of the dinner invitation. Maybe that would be for the best, though. She ignored the disappointment that filled her at the thought. To cover it, she made her voice brisk. "I'll just hang this back up. Did…you want to see my sketches for the other pieces I'm planning for the collection?"

He roused himself out of whatever he'd been thinking and said, "That's not necessary. I'd rather wait until they're completed."

"All right." Joanna was relieved. She often changed her mind from initial sketch to finished product. Sometimes ideas simply didn't work the way she envisioned them, and she had to change direction.

She hung up the pants and halter top, took a deep breath to steady her nerves and turned around. He seemed deep in thought again.

She'd been right. He no longer wanted to take her to dinner. But just as she was about to ask if he'd mind if they skipped dinner because she felt as if she might be coming down with a cold, he looked up, smiled and said, "Are you ready for dinner?"

Joanna wasn't sure what she was ready for where he was concerned. She'd never felt so conflicted about anyone or anything in her life as she felt about him. *This isn't a good idea. Tell him you can feel the onset of a migraine. Tell him anything but yes.* "Actually, I'm starving," she said lightly. "Lunch was a chicken sandwich at my desk."

"Let's go, then. I'm starving myself."

This time when his eyes met hers, there was some emotion in them she couldn't identify. Her heart picked up speed again. Why hadn't she said no to this dinner to begin with? Why had she ignored all the danger signs? Why was she *still* ignoring them? Did she *want* to get her heart broken? For she already sensed the inescapable truth, that if she let down her guard, if she allowed herself to become involved with Marcus on a personal level, and he eventually dumped her, she would be hurt in ways she could only imagine.

It's not too late. Don't go. Just make up an excuse.

Still she said nothing.

And as they walked out into the hallway and she locked the door behind them, she knew that she had crossed over more than her apartment's threshold.

Chapter Nine

Joanna suggested Giacomo's Ristorante, a family-owned, small restaurant two blocks away. "I discovered it shortly after I moved into my apartment, and it's been a favorite ever since."

"Wherever you want to go." He just wanted to be with her.

"They have great food," she went on, "a decent wine list, wonderful service and they're not overpriced."

"Sounds good." She was the first woman he'd ever taken to dinner who had mentioned price. Marcus wasn't sure whether to be amused or impressed. He decided he was impressed and that she'd just gone up another notch in his estimation. Too often over the past years he'd felt as if the women he'd dated cared more for his bottom line and family position than they did for him. Unless Joanna was an extremely good actress, she didn't seem interested in either one.

The two of them covered the short distance to the restaurant in less than ten minutes. Marcus was surprised to discover Joanna walked fast. He hardly had to slow his stride. Amazing, considering how short she was, which meant she probably was taking two steps to his every one. Plus her black leather boots had those ridiculously high heels she seemed to favor, with platforms no less. He figured she wanted to give the illusion of being taller, but how she could navigate in those things was beyond him.

She did look nice, though. He'd thought so from the moment she'd opened her apartment door. She was dressed in a just-above-the-knee flared dark gray skirt and a long black turtleneck sweater worn with a silver belt studded with black onyxlike stones.

At first, he'd wondered if she was going to be warm enough. The evening had turned colder and it felt as if rain was on its way. None was forecast, but this *was* rain country. Once they were outside, he had even suggested she might want to go back and get a raincoat.

"You don't have one," she'd pointed out. "Besides, I'm fine. We don't have far to go." Then she grinned. "If it rains, it won't be the first time I've gotten wet."

Marcus liked the look of the restaurant the minute they walked in the door. It was small, but warm and cozy and softly lit by wall sconces and candles on each table. He also liked that there were white tablecloths and cloth napkins. Lilting accordion music played faintly in the background. A smiling older man with thick white hair and an even thicker accent welcomed them, saying, "*Buonasera,* Miss Joanna and her gentleman friend."

Joanna gave him a warm smile in return. "Giacomo, this is Mr. Barlow."

Giacomo bowed. "It is a pleasure to meet you, Mr. Barlow."

"Thank you." Marcus absorbed the atmosphere. The restaurant was almost two-thirds full, and the diners were dressed casually. He was sorry he hadn't thought to bring a change of clothes to the office today.

"For you, beautiful lady," Giacomo said, "I have a very nice table." He led them to a vacant spot at the front windows that a waiter had just finished clearing and resetting.

"I'm not beautiful," Joanna protested.

"To me you are." Giacomo reached for her hand and kissed it.

To me you are, too, Marcus thought. "You must come here often," he said after they were seated facing each other.

"About once a week, sometimes more than that." She looked sheepish. "I get tired of frozen meals and tuna, and I hate to cook. Besides, who has time?"

Marcus thought of his privileged life. Franny was a terrific cook, and she pampered him. He could always count on having a healthy, delicious meal with no effort on his part. Or his mother's, for that matter.

"It's not as bad as it sounds, though," Joanna continued. "When I'm out, I usually only eat half of my entrée and take the rest home, so I get two meals out of every one. And sometimes three!"

Later, when their entrées arrived, he could see why she'd said that, especially about Giacomo's. The portions served were huge. He'd followed Joanna's recommendation and ordered the Bolognese tagliatelle, which she'd said was considered as authentic as a person could get outside Italy, and he immediately knew there was no way he would eat it all.

She had opted for the chicken marsala. "I love everything here," she confessed. Her dark eyes shone in the candlelight. She laughed softly. "Sometimes I even dream about their food."

If Marcus hadn't known it before, he would have

known in that instant that he was irresistibly drawn to her. There was something so appealing in her enthusiasm, and in how she didn't seem to care about impressing him. In fact, he pretty much liked everything about her now, except for the overdone bohemian clothing she favored and the too much makeup/too much jewelry look. But that could be changed.

Giacomo himself waited on them. When he heard Joanna address Marcus by his first name, he beamed. "You are Italian also!"

Marcus shook his head. "No, I'm not. My mother is French and my father's ancestors came from England. But I'm the third Marcus in the family, so someone way back must have liked the name."

"I think you must have Italian in your blood," Giacomo declared. "That's why our Joanna likes you."

Marcus looked at Joanna, and he could swear she was blushing, but the light was too muted for him to be able to really tell. He couldn't remember when he'd last seen a woman blush. Joanna was full of contradictions. She acted and dressed in an edgy, kind of tough way sometimes, but what you saw was not exactly what you got.

As they ate and talked, he enjoyed watching her. She didn't pick at her food the way so many of the women he'd dated in the past had. The food *was* delicious; Marcus liked it, too. She also seemed to enjoy the excellent Montepulciano he had ordered from the wine list.

Determined to learn as much as he could about her while he had the chance, he said, "You mentioned your family earlier. Do you have siblings?"

She had just cut a piece of chicken and answered before putting it in her mouth, "Four."

"Four!" No one Marcus knew had a large family. "Younger? Older?"

"Tony, Mike and Joey are older. Billy's younger."

"You're the only girl?"

She nodded and twirled some of the spaghetti that had come with her entrée onto her fork.

"Do your brothers worry about you as much as I worry about Vanessa?"

"Unfortunately, I'm afraid they do." The corners of her mouth twitched. "Thankfully, I don't live at home. Neither do any of them, but still...when we get together, I get the third degree, especially from the three that are older." Making a face, she added, "It drives me crazy. Even though I know they just give me a hard time because they care." She popped the forkful of spaghetti into her mouth. A tiny drop of marinara sauce landed on her chin. Not the least bit embarrassed, she blotted it with her napkin.

Her smile was enchanting. Right then, he wanted nothing more than to lean across the table and kiss her. Even the thought of kissing her caused his body to react in areas he'd rather it didn't. At least not while he was in a public place and could do nothing about it.

For the remainder of their meal, he tried to tamp down the growing sexual desire being with her had evoked. He had never liked feeling out of control, and the way he felt about the woman across the table was too much, too soon and too unsettling. He had to be sure he was doing the right thing before he went any further in this relationship, that she really could be the right woman for him, because the one thing he *was* clear about was that Joanna wasn't a woman he could easily walk away from.

Somehow he managed to get through the rest of the meal without doing or saying anything he might be sorry for later.

They both declined coffee or dessert, she had her leftovers boxed and put in a plastic bag and Marcus had just inserted a credit card in the folder containing the check when he noticed the street glittering under the light of a nearby streetlamp. "It's raining," he said.

"I think it just started," Joanna said. "Doesn't seem to be coming down very hard, though."

"I'll go get my car and pick you up outside. That way you won't get wet." He handed the folder to a passing waiter.

"That's not necessary. A little rain won't kill me."

Normally Marcus didn't take no for an answer. Yet when their eyes met across the table, he didn't think he was misreading what he saw in their dark depths. She didn't want the evening to end with him dropping her off at her front door, either—rain or no rain. All the suppressed desire that had flooded him earlier returned.

The rain turned out to be only a light drizzle, so they didn't linger under the awning that sheltered the doorway to Giacomo's. Instead, he put his arm around her protectively, and together they hurried down the street.

In minutes, they reached the corner of her street. They had to cross over and walk several buildings to the east before they'd get to the entrance to her building. The rain was coming down more steadily now, and they had to wait for several cars to pass, but when the street was clear, they dashed across. They had made it up and over the curb when suddenly she slipped and stumbled. He grabbed her with both arms to prevent her from falling down.

The rain, and everything else, faded into the background.

The cars going by, the light from a nearby café, the sound of a siren somewhere in the distance, any possible onlookers—none of these things mattered. Marcus was barely aware of them.

Only the woman he was holding was important.

He tightened his arms around her.

She looked up. Her eyes shone in the dark. The rain had flattened her unruly hair and glistened on her eyelashes. She looked totally beautiful to him.

Without a word or another thought but how much he wanted her, he lowered his head and fitted his mouth to hers.

Joanna's heart went nuts. Despite the rain, despite how wet she now was, despite everything, when his mouth claimed hers, her body felt as if she was having a hot flash. Or at least what she imagined hot flashes felt like.

The kiss—oh, what a kiss!—became two, then three. His tongue delved, he crushed her to him and every part of her—heart, body, brain—responded. If they'd been inside, in her apartment, she would have wanted him to tear off her clothes, to throw her down and have his way with her. She couldn't seem to get close enough. Every fiber of her being wanted, had to have, more.

How long they stood there kissing like two kids who had just awakened to the wonders of sex and couldn't keep their hands off each other, Joanna couldn't have said. Only when someone in a passing car honked the horn several times, with accompanying catcalls, did she reluctantly pull away.

Her head spun from the effect of those kisses, and from the knowledge that he *had* kissed her. She was still breathing hard, and her heart wouldn't slow. She didn't know what to do...or where to look...or what to say.

He seemed just as stunned as she was.

"C'mon," he finally said, putting his arm around her again. "Let's get you inside." His voice sounded gruff and uneven.

Joanna let herself be led. It was only when they entered her building and she saw the shrewd look Thomas gave her that she made a supreme effort to pull herself together enough to say, "The rain caught us walking back from dinner."

"So I see," Thomas said. His normally impassive face had a knowing expression on it.

Joanna kept her head high as she and Marcus went to the elevator and pushed the button to summon it. Screw Thomas. Who cared what he thought? All she cared about was what Marcus thought. Even after the elevator doors closed and they were on the way to the fifth floor, he didn't say anything. She bit her lip. He didn't look at her, either.

Was he sorry?

Oh, God.

He probably *was* sorry. Maybe he even thought she'd only pretended to fall so he'd have to catch her. That she'd somehow *planned* what had happened next.

She swallowed.

Well, if he was sorry, she guessed she'd soon know. And she'd handle it. No matter what it cost her.

He'd done it now, Marcus thought as he followed Joanna into her apartment. Instead of using caution and making a rational decision, he'd jumped right smack into the danger zone. There was no going back.

Did he want to go back?

Kissing Joanna had only intensified his desire for her, yet he knew it was too soon for more. He didn't know her well enough yet, and he couldn't afford or deal with another mistake and the emotional upheaval it caused, for he wasn't cold enough or calculated enough to just walk away without caring whom he might have hurt. This time, and especially with this woman, he had to be damn sure. And he couldn't be that positive until he'd had enough time alone to think about what had already happened between them tonight.

To make a rational decision, not one ruled by his hormones.

He shouldn't even have come up to the apartment. He should have said good-night at the door, then made certain she was safely inside.

But how could he have done that without at least mentioning what had happened between them? He couldn't pretend he hadn't kissed her like a starving man.

He was still trying to figure out what to say to make a graceful exit when she turned around and, meeting his gaze with something very close to dignity, said, "Marcus, I think we need to cool it, don't you?"

Relief and disappointment warred for dominance. Now he wanted nothing more than to yank her back into his arms and kiss her senseless and after that, to lead her into her bedroom and show her how much he did *not* want to cool it.

But something about her expression warned him he'd better not start something he couldn't finish, something that might ruin everything for both of them. He'd better be sensible and rational and very, very sure about his feelings for her and where lovemaking between them would ultimately lead before he leaped... again.

Regretfully, he nodded. "You're right." He refused to say he was sorry, because he wasn't, and he didn't want her to think he was. Showing someone you found her desirable wasn't a sin. Going forward if you weren't serious would be, especially with a woman like Joanna.

Bending forward, he kissed her cheek. "Good night, Joanna. Thank you for a wonderful evening." He smiled at her. "Now go get dry. I'll feel guilty if you catch a cold."

Without waiting for her to answer, he turned and walked out the door.

When the door closed behind him, Joanna began to shiver uncontrollably. A minute later her face was wet with something other than rain.

She'd been right.

He *was* sorry.

Thank God she hadn't made a fool of herself by showing him how bereft she felt right now and how much she'd wanted him to contradict her and say he didn't agree, that he wanted them to make love. Tonight. She closed her eyes. Those kisses! How could he have kissed her like that if he *didn't* want to make love to her?

Why was she so stupid?

Why hadn't she backed away? She'd *known* he was going to kiss her. She could have stopped him.

You didn't want to.

No. She hadn't wanted to. And, being a man, he had taken what he wanted in the moment. If the same thing had happened here in her apartment, they probably would have gone on to the next step, and then, when he'd had a chance to think about it afterward, and realized he'd made a big mistake, she'd have been in a lot worse predicament. Because kiss or no kiss, romp in bed or no romp in bed, she still had to see Marcus if she wanted the show in his gallery.

Now her disappointment and emptiness morphed into anger. Not at Marcus. Anger at herself. *Grow up. You knew any romantic relationship with Marcus would never work out. So why are you so unhappy?*

She should be thanking the Lord that Marcus had seen it, too, and that he'd made it easy for her to extricate herself from a no-win situation. If he'd tried to apologize or say what had happened had been a mistake, she'd have died. As it was, her pride and her dignity were intact.

This disappointment was just a blip on her horizon.

She would get over it.

Wouldn't she?

Chapter Ten

Joanna and her mother spent most of Saturday looking at rentals. Georgie had recommended a real estate
agent her family knew, and the woman, incongru-
ously named Bunny—"It's not short for anything. My
mother just liked the name!"—was a whiz who lived
up to Georgie's description of a go-getter who knew
her business.

Still, the whole process took time. A couple of the
listings Bunny showed them were pretty good—not
perfect, but acceptable—and Joanna could have been
content with either, but she still wanted to see everything available before making a final decision. If she
didn't, she'd always wonder if she had missed out on
the perfect place.

A few minutes after three, she found it.

The space, a large storefront that was already di-
vided between the front area, which was a perfect size
for the kind of showroom she wanted, and a much
larger back area, where she and a couple of assistants
could have an ideal workroom. There was also another
small room behind the workroom that could serve as
an office or even a storage room if she wanted her office to be private, as well as a kitchen and a bathroom.
Plus, there was an apartment on the second level with

two bedrooms! The second could be turned into anything Joanna wanted. She could use it for her private office or even just a creative haven away from everything and everyone.

And unbelievably, the rental space was located in Belltown, only blocks from Marcus's gallery. It was an ideal neighborhood, both for commerce and for living. Why, she could even walk to the Pike Place Market if she wanted to, and the Queen Anne area, where Georgie had grown up, was also within walking distance. In addition, there was a public parking lot nearby, so her customers wouldn't have to hassle with street parking if they didn't want to. And by leasing the space, she would get two parking slots in a garage next door, so she'd be covered.

Joanna could hardly believe it when she got her first look at the listing. They were asking more than she had wanted to pay, but she knew, even without Bunny telling her, that the location and space were worth it.

"We *could* offer a little less," Bunny said in answer to Joanna's unspoken query, "but I doubt they'll agree. This really is prime space, Joanna. It just came on the market, and someone's bound to snap it up soon."

"It does seem perfect," Ann Marie said. "The only thing is…"

Joanna frowned. "What?"

"It's not secure like where you live now. Your dad and I, we'll worry."

"She can install a good alarm system," Bunny interjected quickly. "She'd want to do that with any ground-floor space. And she can put a double lock on the door at the foot of the stairs leading to the apartment, so she'll have extra security that way, too."

"I'll be perfectly safe," Joanna said. Then she grinned. "I can get a dog!" She'd always wanted a dog. She loved her cat, Tabitha, but she'd always dreamed of having a German shepherd like the one her doctor had kept in her office for years as a mascot/guard/companion.

"Well…" her mother said, obviously weakening. "I guess your Dad might feel okay about this place if you had a dog."

It was on the tip of Joanna's tongue to say that she was too old for her father to still think he could make her decisions for her and hadn't they settled that a long time ago? But she restrained herself—why upset her mother?—and said instead, "I'll take it, Bunny."

Bunny smiled happily. "I'll call the listing agent right now. Cross your fingers he hasn't already gotten a contract on it."

Now that she'd seen this space, Joanna knew she would be very disappointed if she didn't get it. So she not only crossed her fingers, she said a few Hail Marys while Bunny placed the call.

In the meantime, Joanna's mother was walking around, inspecting everything and making notes on a little pad she always carried in her purse. "You're going to need more electrical outlets in the back room, Joanna. We'll get Uncle Walt to do that for you." Joanna's uncle Walt, an electrician, was married to her mother's younger sister, Tessie. "And our Mike can install some blinds you can pull down to close off those big front windows at night."

Joanna's gaze met Bunny's, and Bunny winked. She was currently on hold at the listing agency. "Mom,"

Joanna said, "I should hire you to run my business for me."

Ann Marie looked up from her notes. "And if I didn't have the yarn shop, I'd jump at the chance!"

Joanna was afraid to think too far ahead in case something went wrong, because Bunny was still on hold, but her mind spun. Oh, if this place already had a contract on it, she didn't know what she'd do. None of the others she'd looked at could hold a candle to this one, and she knew now that she'd seen it, she wouldn't be happy with anything else.

Finally Bunny was connected to the listing agent. After telling him Joanna wanted the place and she would be sending the contract over within the hour, she listened for a few seconds, then gave Joanna a broad smile and a thumbs-up.

Yes! Joanna almost forgot how miserable she'd been the night before as she and her mother hugged each other and Joanna did a little happy dance. But once the contract was signed and Joanna had written a check to accompany it, and Bunny had said she'd email Joanna a final copy from the listing agency and then taken them back to Joanna's apartment, where her mother kissed her goodbye and said to call her if she needed anything, Joanna's spirits flagged a bit.

Yesterday, BTK (before the kiss!), she'd have immediately called Marcus to tell him the good news. But now, after the way he'd left her, she knew she wasn't going to have that pleasure. Oh, she'd tell him about the space once she had the finalized contract in hand, but she'd do it during business hours and it would be in the form of an email.

Because those kisses and, afterward, the way he'd

so quickly agreed they needed to cool it, had changed everything.

She had learned her lesson.

She wasn't going to spin daydreams about him anymore.

Their relationship was going back to being about business only, because she had no intention of ending up with a broken heart.

Marcus spent Saturday morning at the gallery. Brenda didn't work weekends unless something special was going on. Instead, a young graduate student named Peter Truby manned the showroom floor. He was a nice kid. Normally when Marcus was there, he enjoyed talking to Peter. Today, though, Marcus spent most of his time back in the office where he had intended to look at the financials and pay some bills.

But he was finding it hard to concentrate today. His thoughts kept turning to Friday night and everything that had transpired between him and Joanna. He wasn't happy with the way he'd conducted himself or with the way the evening had ended. He knew her suggestion that they cool it was a sensible one, but he couldn't help wishing he hadn't been so quick to agree. Why hadn't he asked her why she felt that way? Why had he been so rattled that he said okay and then just left?

Because you lost control.

Yes. That was the crux of the problem. He'd lost control, done something without thinking of the consequences and whether he was ready for them, and it had unsettled him.

Dammit, anyway.

He couldn't help feeling he'd acted like a jerk.

And he wasn't a jerk. In fact, he prided himself on being a gentleman, someone who always conducted himself in a way that would have made his father proud.

Marcus was still trying to decide what action, if any, he might take to try to make amends without also looking like a fool when his cell phone rang and the name Jamison Wells showed on the display.

"Hello, Jamison," he said, pleased to hear from the artist.

"Hello, Marcus. Sorry to bother you on the weekend, but I wanted to let you know I'm coming into Seattle Monday and will be bringing as many of my finished paintings as I can fit in the car."

Marcus smiled. He had been wanting to talk to Jamison in person rather than try to explain what he envisioned for his exhibition, especially what he was planning for the show where Joanna's and Vanessa's work would also be showcased, and now he'd have the opportunity sooner than he'd expected. "No problem. I'm at the gallery this morning."

"I was hoping I could meet that woman whose fashions are going to be shown along with my work," Jamison continued.

"Absolutely," Marcus said. "She's anxious to meet you, too. How long are you planning to be in town?" Jamison lived in Anacortes, which was about an hour-and-a-half drive, sometimes more, depending on traffic.

"I can stay the night if I have to."

"If you want to meet Joanna, you might have to. She's working out a notice and probably won't be able to get away from her office before five."

"Okay. I'll plan to spend the night, then. Got any

recommendations about a place to stay that isn't too far from the gallery? Or too expensive?"

Marcus thought for a minute. "Tell you what. You can use the Barlow company's corporate suite. The one we keep for visiting VIPs. No one is scheduled to be there all week, so it's free and it's only about fifteen minutes from here."

"That would be great."

"Consider it done, then."

"I'll come straight to the gallery, and you can show me how to get to the suite when we wrap up on Monday."

Marcus checked his calendar, saw that Monday afternoon was blessedly free of appointments at work. "I'm free in the afternoon Monday. I can be here by one."

After they'd hung up, Marcus realized Jamison's call had given him the perfect reason to contact Joanna again without it being awkward. He still didn't know what he'd do going forward, but at least the first part of his problem was solved.

On Monday morning Joanna was in the middle of showing Lonnie how to process a new order when a call came in from Marcus's assistant, Judith Holmes.

"Ms. Spinelli," she said, "Mr. Barlow is tied up on an international call and asked me to phone you."

Even though Joanna was only talking to his assistant, her stupid heart still thumped harder. God, she was a mess. No wonder she attracted losers like Chick instead of the kind of man she hoped to someday find.

"He wanted me to tell you," the Holmes woman continued, "that Jamison Wells will be in town and at the gallery this afternoon. Mr. Wells is anxious to meet you, and Mr. Barlow wondered if you could come to the gallery after you finish work."

Joanna knew she couldn't refuse. Nor did she want to. She was anxious herself to meet the artist with whom she'd be sharing her big night. Plus she couldn't help wondering how Marcus would react when they were together again, and this was an ideal way to find out—when someone else would be there to act as a buffer between them. Her only concern was her own ability to stay cool and confident and professional, yet friendly and warm enough so that Jamison Wells would like her.

Piece of cake, Georgie would say.

Yeah, right, Joanna thought.

But her tone didn't convey her doubts when she agreed that yes, she could be at the gallery no later than five-thirty. She would even leave a few minutes early to ensure that there would be no problems. Lonnie might as well learn how to lock up herself. She would have to be doing it next week anyway.

"Mr. Barlow was hoping you might have your portfolio with you," Judith Holmes said before they hung up. "He knows Mr. Wells would like to see it."

"I always carry it with me," Joanna said. She'd gotten into that habit long ago, because another of her mother's favorite pieces of advice was that you never knew when opportunity would come knocking, and you should always be ready.

For the rest of the day, part of Joanna's brain was engaged by something other than Lonnie's training. Instead, it was firmly centered on the upcoming meeting at the gallery. And, of course, from time to time, especially when Marcus entered her thoughts, that stupid heart of hers would give a little flip just to let her know no matter how many times she told herself she could see Marcus again without letting it affect her emotionally, her heart might not have gotten the message.

Marcus was nervous. And he didn't like that feeling, either. What the hell was it about Joanna that had so strongly affected him? He only hoped his ability to keep his emotions hidden from public view wouldn't desert him today.

When Joanna walked into the gallery a few minutes after five-thirty, he wasn't sure he'd be able to pull it off. Just looking at her—the way her hair had gotten blown by the wind and was even messier than usual, the way her dark eyes met his for one naked moment before moving to Jamison, who stood beside him, and the way it seemed to take an effort for her to smile as naturally as she had Friday night before he'd kissed her—all reminded him more forcefully than words or any lectures he might have given himself that he might already have crossed into territory he'd never been in before. That maybe it was too late to go backward.

Today she was dressed more like the first day he'd seen her—in a black velvet miniskirt, black-patterned tights, those granny boots of hers, paired with a form-fitting woven, glittery silver top over which she'd slung a black capelike jacket. Huge silver disks dangled from her ears, and both arms sported a combination of silver and black bracelets. If he hadn't known she'd learned about this meeting a short while ago, he might have thought she'd purposely dressed defiantly, because her makeup was exaggerated even more than usual, topped off with black lipstick. Was she trying to tell him something? Surely she'd guessed he liked her in more conservative clothing. He'd certainly complimented her enough when she'd exhibited less attention-getting outfits and appearance.

Regardless, if Jamison hadn't been right there, Marcus might have forgotten everything he wanted to change about her and pulled down the front shades, locked the door and carried her off to the leather sofa in his office, where he could easily have removed the in-your-face clothes and jewelry and done what his body was telling him might be useless to fight.

Truth was, he still wanted her.

Badly.

But Jamison *was* here. And Joanna was walking toward them. Now her smile was wide and friendly. And it was directed at Jamison.

Marcus looked at Jamison, too. What he saw rocked him, possibly more than he was already rocked by his own reaction to Joanna. For Jamison looked as if he'd been hit by a truck. His expression seemed stunned. There was no other word for it.

"You must be the wonderful artist I'm going to have the privilege of sharing a show with," Joanna was saying. She gave Jamison her right hand to shake as well as an admiring smile. "It's such a pleasure to meet you. I'm Joanna."

"The pleasure is all mine," Jamison said. He kept hold of Joanna's hand and bent down and kissed her cheek. "Marcus didn't tell me you were so beautiful."

Marcus stiffened. For the first time in many years, he couldn't think of a thing to say.

Unlike when Giacomo had called Joanna beautiful, she didn't contradict Jamison. Instead, she said, "And he didn't tell *me* you were such a charmer." She laughed softly. "I expected some scruffy old guy with paint on his clothes, not someone like you."

They were flirting with each other! Right in front of him! Marcus wondered if they'd forgotten he was even there in the throes of their mutual admiration society.

He cleared his throat. "I see you brought your portfolio," he said to Joanna in the most cool and collected tone he could muster. "Why don't you put it down and we'll go into the back and you can see the paintings Jamison brought in today."

Joanna beamed. But not at Marcus. At Jamison. She practically batted her eyelashes at him. Was she doing this on purpose? Marcus wondered. Was she *trying* to make him jealous? He'd never been jealous over a woman a day in his life.

And he wasn't jealous now.

He was just disgusted, that's all. Couldn't these two restrain themselves? Jamison was practically salivating; he couldn't take his eyes off her. And she was lapping it up, like a kitten attacking a bowl of cream. Next thing he knew, Jamison would be asking her for a date. And going by the way she was looking at the younger man, she would say yes.

This wasn't going to work.

It wasn't going to work at all.

Maybe Brenda had been right. Maybe Marcus should never have thought about combining the shows of these two. Huh. Maybe he shouldn't have ever given Joanna a show at all.

Well, it wasn't too late to change his mind.

Chapter Eleven

Joanna couldn't believe how well things had gone today. She needn't have worried about seeing Marcus again. Jamison Wells being at the gallery had changed everything. His reaction to her, the way he so obviously liked and admired her, had given her a much-needed ego boost. And when he'd held her hand as they parted and asked if he could call her, saying he didn't live that far away at all, that some of the people who lived in Anacortes actually commuted to Seattle on a daily basis, he had made her feel as if she really *were* beautiful and desirable and someone *he'd* never just walk away from.

"Maybe I could come into town and take you to dinner or lunch on a weekend," he'd suggested.

"That would be lovely," she'd answered in return. She'd sneaked a quick peek at Marcus and was totally satisfied to see the almost imperceptible tightening of his lips. He didn't like the way she and Jamison were acting. Well, wasn't that just too bad?

Feeling a surge of power, she'd smiled at Jamison even more warmly, and when he then suggested she might like to come up to Anacortes and see his studio and that he'd love to visit her workroom, she'd warmly agreed to both. The look on Marcus's face then had been priceless. He'd tried to hide what he was feeling, but Joanna knew he was furious. She'd seen that same expression when he got mad at Vanessa. Good. She hoped he was upset! Did he think he was the only man who had ever looked at her twice?

She told Jamison she'd be looking forward to his call and took out one of her business cards. Before handing it to him, she wrote her cell phone number on the back.

Then she politely thanked Marcus, gave Jamison another I-really-like-you smile and said goodbye. Her only regret was she couldn't see Marcus's reaction or hear what he said to Jamison once she was gone. Now she was on her way to the parking lot where she'd left her car.

Oh, it felt good to know Marcus wasn't as cool as she'd first imagined. The fact that Jamison was young and handsome and such a talented artist sure didn't hurt. Knowing how Marcus had had to give up his dreams of a career as an artist, she felt a pang of remorse for the hurt she must have caused him today.

And yet that was ridiculous, wasn't it? She had no reason to feel bad. Marcus didn't want her. He'd walked away without a backward glance. So today he'd gotten exactly what he deserved. To hell with Marcus Barlow.

But the moment *that* thought formed, she stopped short, almost causing a man walking behind her to crash into her.

"Jeez, lady," he said, "watch what you're doing!"

"Sorry," Joanna said. Watch what she was doing? She'd better watch what she was *thinking*. She couldn't say to hell with Marcus Barlow. He was her benefactor. He was giving her a huge opportunity. How could she forget that fact, even for a second?

Was she losing her mind?

So it was flattering that someone as appealing as Jamison Wells had found her attractive. But did she have to rub Marcus's nose in it by gushing all over the artist? While he was watching?

Suddenly clear-eyed, Joanna knew she'd better be careful. When dealing with Marcus, she'd better always be aware that he wasn't just some guy she was dating. He was the man who was giving her the chance to show her work to the movers and shakers in Seattle society. For she had no doubt that most of Marcus's crowd would come to her show, if only because of him and his sister.

What was more important?

Making a point with Marcus?

Or the opportunity of a lifetime in terms of her dreams and goals?

All of Joanna's elation over Jamison Wells and his reaction to her disappeared as if it had never been. She just prayed she hadn't totally blown everything today.

After Joanna left the gallery, Marcus didn't have to wonder what Jamison was thinking, because the man couldn't stop talking. And every other word out of his mouth contained her name.

"I didn't see a ring on her finger," he said. "And she didn't say no when I suggested getting together, so I don't think she's involved with anyone. Do you?"

"I wouldn't know," Marcus said stiffly.

"She would have said so, don't you think?"

Marcus shrugged. He had no intention of encouraging Jamison's juvenile infatuation with Joanna. To halt his nonstop raving about her, Marcus said, "I'm getting hungry. You ready for dinner?"

"Sounds good," Jamison said.

Marcus suggested a Thai restaurant close to the building where the corporate suite was located. The food there was excellent; plus, the restaurant had the added benefit of a decent-sized parking lot. Jamison followed Marcus in his car, and after they were inside the restaurant and had placed their orders, they discussed the paintings Jamison had brought to the gallery that day and what Marcus had planned in terms of advertising and promotion.

Their discussion continued through most of their dinner and Marcus had finally relaxed and begun to enjoy himself when Jamison said, "You probably think I'm nuts, but I can't stop thinking about Joanna." He smiled sheepishly. "You've known her longer. Do you have any advice for me?"

Marcus drank some of his wine to give him time to think. "You probably don't want to hear this, but it's never a good idea to mix business with pleasure." *What a hypocrite you are.*

Jamison nodded. "I know that, but…she's really special…don't you think?"

Now what could Marcus say? Without being a liar as well as a hyprocrite? "She's definitely unusual." He tried to keep his tone noncommital.

Jamison frowned. "Don't you like her? Is there something I should know?"

Marcus had always prided himself on being both honest and fair. And Jamison was too nice a guy, and Marcus had too much respect for him, to be anything less. "Sorry, I didn't mean to give that impression. As far as I know, she's a very nice person."

Jamison smiled. "Even if you'd said she wasn't, it wouldn't have stopped me calling her." His smile got broader. "A guy doesn't meet someone like her every day."

Even after they'd said good-night and Marcus was on his way home, he couldn't get Jamison's last comment out of his mind. *A guy doesn't meet someone like her every day.*

Marcus knew he had to do something.

The question was, did he want Joanna or not? What if he waited too long while he was trying to make up his mind and she and Jamison hooked up?

Maybe that would be for the best. Maybe Jamison was better for her. After all, he was part of her world, a real artist, not a wannabe like Marcus.

Joanna didn't care about Marcus's money, he already knew that, and his position and family were probably a detriment with her, not an advantage.

What do I have to offer her? A life she probably doesn't want and wouldn't enjoy. A life I'm stuck with and see no hope of changing anytime soon. Is that fair?

Marcus knew the right thing, the sensible thing, would be to stand aside and allow whatever developed between Jamison and Joanna to develop without Marcus's interference.

But was he strong enough to do that?

Could he really step aside and watch the woman he wanted more than he'd ever wanted a woman before hook up with the artist he already secretly envied?

* * *

Joanna had just settled down to watch TV for a while when her cell rang. She didn't recognize the number, but answered anyway.

"Joanna? It's Jamison Wells."

Wishing she'd thought harder about what she'd say to him, she muted the television set and said brightly, "Well, hi. I didn't expect to hear from you again so soon."

"I haven't been able to think about much else but calling you ever since you left the gallery today," he said.

Joanna swallowed. Why did he have to be so nice? And why had she been so stupid as to get involved with Marcus on anything but a business level? "That's an awfully nice thing to say."

"It's the truth. I—I've never met anyone like you."

"I know I'm a bit odd. My mother says so all the time," Joanna said in an attempt to lighten the conversation.

"You're not odd. You're…wonderful."

Joanna felt like crying. If only Marcus was on the other end of the phone. If only he was the one saying such sweet things. "Jamison, look, I really appreciate—"

"Don't say it," he interrupted. "Don't blow me off. I mean everything I said. It's not a line."

Yes, she knew he meant it. She could hear the sincerity in his voice. She'd seen the admiration in his eyes. He was a straight arrow. That was the problem. If he was handing her a line, she'd have no problem turning him down.

"I know it's not a line," she said gently.

"I really like you. I—I want us to get to know each other better."

When she would have responded, he quickly said, "Wait, don't say anything yet. Let me finish."

Joanna sighed, but quietly, so he wouldn't hear her. "Okay."

"I've decided to stay in town this week. Marcus told me the company suite—that's where I'm staying—is free all week and I don't think he'll care if I use it. I thought maybe we could spend some time together and get to know each other…and just see how we feel."

"The thing is," Joanna said, "I'm working out a notice at my day job and I'll be tied up all day through Friday. And at night, I need to work on my designs as well as get ready to move." She explained about the new place she'd rented over the weekend. "I'm not going to have time to go out and do fun things."

"I don't mind watching you work. In fact, I'd really like that."

"I can't really work on my designs with an audience." This was true. Joanna worked best on her own. She was even a bit worried about how it would be to have helpers. Sometimes it was a real hindrance to be such a control freak.

"I wouldn't say a word. I'd just watch."

"Jamison, you're so nice, I—"

"C'mon, Joanna, give a guy a break. I promise I won't bother you. I won't make a sound. I'll just sit in the corner and read a book until you need a break."

"I'm sorry. I can't. Maybe after the show is over and I have some free time again, we can see how we feel. By then, you may have changed your mind about me." She laughed. "I wouldn't be at all surprised if you did."

"I won't change my mind."

Joanna forced herself not to say anything else.

After a long moment of silence, he finally sighed heavily. "All right. I understand. I can't work with someone watching me, either, and I know you're under pressure right now. This is your first big show, isn't it?"

"Yes, it is. And it's very, very important to me."

"Yeah. I understand that, too."

"Thank you."

"But I won't change my mind, Joanna. I'm going to hold you to it. Just as soon as your show is over, I'm going to keep after you until you say yes."

And maybe by then, she'd be able to. Maybe she would no longer hold out hope that something would change between her and Marcus.

"You're a sweet guy," she said.

"And you're an amazing woman."

Later, as Joanna was brushing her teeth in preparation for bed, she thought about her conversation with Jamison again. She wished…oh, she didn't know what she wished. She only knew that it would be much better for her if Marcus had never kissed her and she had never kissed him back. Those kisses and the way they made her feel had complicated her life at a time when she should be thinking about fabrics and silhouettes, not a man she knew was wrong for her in every way.

Marcus couldn't fall asleep.

Disgusted with himself, he finally got up, fixed himself a stiff drink and switched on the TV. He hadn't watched late-night TV in years, but tonight he knew he had to do something to distract himself. And to get Joanna out of his mind.

Unfortunately for him, the first person he saw when he turned on the TV was the actress Marion Cotillard, and something about her gamine look and dark intensity reminded him so strongly of Joanna that he felt a stirring in his loins.

Oh, for crying out loud! Finishing his drink, he switched off the television set. Christ, he was a mess. He couldn't believe he'd let a woman get under his skin like this.

It wasn't until he was back in bed and finally drifting off to sleep that he knew what he needed to do.

And he would do it tomorrow.

At eleven o'clock Joanna texted Georgie. Are U asleep?

No, she texted back. Drinking warm milk and reading. What's up?

I need advice. Can U call me?

Give me a minute.

Five minutes later, Joanna's cell rang. After explaining everything to Georgie, Joanna said, "I don't know what to do."

"I think you already did it."

"What do you mean?"

"Well, knowing you and how stubborn you are, if you really liked this Jamison guy and wanted to go out with him, you would have found some time for him."

"Yes, but what I meant is, I don't know what to do *now*."

"About Marcus, you mean?"

"Yes."

"Tell me something, Joanna. Are you in love with him?"

Joanna huffed out a breath. "I don't know. I...I might be."

"That means you probably are."

"Yeah, I know."

"Well, then..."

"Well, then, what?"

"Oh, c'mon. The Joanna I know goes after what she wants. She doesn't sit around waiting for something to happen. If you love Marcus and you want him, why in the world did you tell him you thought you should cool it? Why didn't you go for the brass ring?"

"You know why, Georgie. I didn't want to make a fool of myself. I mean, what if we'd had sex and then he decided he didn't want me after all?"

"So you were scared."

"Well...yes."

"Hon, we're all scared. Falling in love is darned scary. For everybody. I mean, it's like you're standing on this high cliff and you have to leap. Falling in love is giving someone else control over you. It's gambling. It's a whole load of scary stuff. But if you don't take the chance, if you don't leap, you'll never know what might have happened."

Joanna bit her lip.

"So I think you do know what to do. The question is, are you brave enough to do it?"

"Am I doing something wrong?" Lonnie asked. Her hazel eyes were worried.

"Huh?" Joanna had been off in daydream-land

somewhere. It was Tuesday morning and she and Lonnie were going over the books.

"You just seem distracted, or something. I was afraid maybe you didn't know how to tell me I'm not doing things right."

"Oh, Lonnie, I'm sorry. It's not you. You're doing great. I—I just have a lot on my mind right now."

Lonnie gave her a long look. "Guy trouble?" she finally asked.

Joanna smiled crookedly. "Is it that obvious?"

Lonnie shrugged. "You did kind of have that glazed look in your eyes."

"Sorry. And yes, I was thinking about a guy."

"Want to talk about it?"

"Not really. I don't want to even be thinking about it, but I can't seem to stop myself."

"Yeah, I've been there, too." Lonnie grimaced. "I have horrible judgment when it comes to guys."

"That's my problem, too. I got involved with someone I shouldn't have and then he dumped me and now I seem to be doing the same thing."

"What do you mean, you shouldn't have? Was he married or something?"

"Oh, God, no," Joanna said. "I'm not *that* stupid. I'd never do a thing like that." She almost said he was someone she worked with, but stopped herself at the last moment. "Listen, I don't want to take valuable time I need to use on your training to talk about myself and my love life…or lack thereof. It's too boring, anyway."

For the rest of the morning, Joanna made a determined effort to keep both Jamison Wells and Marcus Barlow out of her thoughts. It was hard, but she managed. And as a result, she and Lonnie got a lot accomplished. So she was feeling pretty good about her day and her guard was down when her cell phone rang a few minutes past noon. The display showed Barlow International as the caller. Thinking it was Judith Holmes again—she seemed to be the one to call when Marcus had a message for Joanna—she was totally unprepared to hear Marcus's voice.

"Oh," she said. "I—I didn't know—" She broke off abruptly. She sounded like an idiot.

"I hope I'm not interrupting anything important," he said.

"No, no, I'm just having lunch."

"I won't keep you long."

"It's okay." Her heart was doing its stupid flip-flop thing again. What the heck was her *problem?* Couldn't she control herself?

"The reason I'm calling is I wanted to invite you to accompany me to the Hooper Women's Shelter Benefit Dinner Dance Friday night."

Joanna was so stunned that for a moment she couldn't answer. "You want *me* to go with you?"

"Yes. I think it would be a really great opportunity for you to meet potential clients. My mother and sister will also be going."

His mother and sister would *also* be going? Joanna's head spun.

"You can't buy this kind of exposure," he added.

"I—realize that. I guess I'm just surprised, that's all."

"Surprised? Why is that?"

"B-because I… Oh, I don't know. I… Thank you. I'd be happy to go with you." *Ohmigod.* What would she wear? She'd have to whip something up, and fast.

"Good. I'll pick you up at six-fifteen. The benefit starts at seven, but since I'm one of the sponsors, I'd like to be there early."

"Okay."

"That's not a problem for you? I realize Friday's your last day at the office."

"It's not a problem. The office closes at four on Fridays."

"Good. And, Joanna?"

"Yes?"

"It's a formal evening. And you should think about wearing one of your designs."

Joanna almost snorted. Almost. She caught herself in time. "I was just thinking the very same thing," she said.

"All right. I'll see you then."

It took a long time for her heart to settle into a normal pattern again. And an even longer time for Joanna to put the phone call out of her mind so she could concentrate on work for the rest of the day.

Chapter Twelve

The rest of the week flew by for Joanna. She spent her days training Lonnie and her nights hurriedly piecing together, ripping apart and redoing an evening dress to wear to the benefit on Friday. In between, she fielded calls from Jamison Wells—he certainly was persistent!—made to-do lists, complained to Georgie, tried not to think about Marcus and worried about how she'd ever find the time to move and/or hire an assistant.

Georgie, in true BFF fashion, offered to come and help.

"Help?" Joanna said. "How can you come and help? You've got a job of your own, not to mention a husband, three stepchildren and a baby on the way. Don't be ridiculous. Good grief, Zach will kill me if you even suggest it."

"It was Zach's idea," Georgie said.

"You're kidding." No man was *that* perfect.

"Nope. He thinks I need some time away from the rat race."

"So you're going to trade one rat race for another?" Joanna said, shaking her head.

Georgie chuckled. "It's different when it's someone else's rat race. No stress, just the fun of helping."

"Oh, Georgie, I'd love to have you, and I know your

mother would be thrilled to see you, but I can't let you do that. I'm sorry I was whining. It's not fair to you to dump my problems on your shoulders."

"My shoulders are pretty broad." Georgie's voice softened. "And you're my best friend. Let me help. I want to."

After that, what could Joanna say? "Well, it *would* be wonderful. Will you stay with me?" Where would she put Georgie? It wasn't as if she had an extra bed. Or even *one* bed.

"I won't go that far. Pregnant women need good beds. No, I'll stay at my mom's, but I'll be there every day. I'm a very good sorter and packer. Exactly when are you moving?"

"I had to give thirty days' notice here, but I'm moving as soon as I can get organized. I hoped to start this coming weekend. I have to pay rent at both places anyway, so why not have more room? Then maybe I can get someone hired to help me and things'll be easier."

"I can definitely help you do that," Georgie pointed out. "I'll make a few phone calls. We'll find you the perfect assistant."

After they hung up, Joanna thought how lucky she was to have Georgie as her best friend.

Joanna's mother also offered to help, and Joanna gratefully accepted. In fact, her mother ended up coming over on Thursday night and hemming the gown Joanna would wear the following evening.

"Oh, Joanna, this is so beautiful," her mother said as she fingered the delicate lace. "Will you put it in your show?"

"I can't really dress anyone else in it, Mom. I don't

know a single model who's as short as I am. But I can wear it for the show, don't you think?"

Ann Marie smiled. "I think that would be perfect." She held the dress up to the light. "You've done a wonderful job on it. I can't believe you designed and made this in just three days." Her voice softened. "You're so talented, honey. And I'm so proud of you."

Joanna swallowed against a lump in her throat. She walked over, leaned down and hugged her mother. "I love you, Mom."

But the tender moment didn't last long, for a few seconds later, Ann Marie said, "Now tell me about this Marcus Barlow. Are you dating him? Or is this strictly a business thing tomorrow night?"

"I told you, Mom," Joanna said, careful to keep her voice noncommittal, "he said the benefit would be a perfect opportunity for me to meet the kind of women I hope to have as clients."

"Yes, I know, but are you *dating* him?"

Her mother's eyes were altogether too shrewd as they studied her. Joanna knew she'd better be honest without giving away too much. The last thing she wanted was her mother worrying about her any more than she already did. "Not really. He's taken me to dinner once or twice, but it's pretty much been about business." *Oh, right. Those kisses were so business-like, weren't they?*

"Hmm. Okay." Ann Marie didn't look convinced.

"He's not my type. More to the point, I'm not his."

"What do you mean?"

"He's wealthy. He comes from an old Seattle family. And he's so conservative he makes Uncle Walt seem like a liberal." Uncle Walt was the family's ultraconservative member. "And you know how I am...."

"Yes, I know how you are. You're a beautiful, talented, wonderful young woman, and any man would be lucky to get you!" her mother said loyally. "Don't you *ever* start thinking you're not good enough. You're good enough for *anyone*."

"You're prejudiced," Joanna said. She couldn't help laughing at her mother's vehemence, although she was touched. She had always known she could count on her mother, even when Ann Marie was driving her crazy. That certainty had been the mainstay of her life.

"Maybe so, but I'm only telling the truth. And if this Marcus Barlow has any taste at all, he'll see the truth, too."

Joanna smiled, but inside she knew that Marcus Barlow had already seen the truth, and the truth was that they made a great combination when it came to their business partnership, but personally was another story. Her mother could say she was good enough for anyone, but Joanna knew she would never fit into Marcus's life. She would be miserable pretending to be something she wasn't, and eventually he would be miserable, too.

Long after her mother had gone home, and the black-lace gown was hanging safely out of harm's way—meaning Tabitha's curious paws—Joanna lay in bed and told herself not to forget that truth.

Because forgetting would be the road to heartbreak.

Marcus's eyes widened at the sight of Joanna wearing a spectacular black-lace evening gown. She looked amazing. There was no other word for it. Her curvy figure was shown to clear advantage in the softly draped dress with a plunging neckline and halterlike top. Her hair hadn't been tamed, but its black spikes were softened by the addition of a beautiful red silk flower positioned over her left ear and sparkling jet earrings that dangled daintily from her ears. Her makeup was more subdued, too, although not around the eyes, which were—if anything—even more smoky and dramatically outlined than usual. Tonight she wore a vivid red lipstick that matched the flower, but he noticed her nail polish was still black. That fact almost amused him. Silver sandals with very high heels and a small beaded black purse completed her outfit.

"You look beautiful," he said.

"Thank you." She smiled, but the smile didn't reach her eyes. "I made the dress."

"Yes, I thought so."

"So you like it?"

Liking it was an understatement. The dress was sexy and elegant at the same time, something he imagined was very hard to pull off. No doubt about it. She was a talented designer. "I like it very much."

"Do you think the women I'll meet tonight will like it, too?"

"I think, once they know you're a designer, they'll be lining up to order their own dresses."

Her smile finally seemed genuine. "I hope you're right."

"You're going to be cold," he said when she picked up her purse and seemed ready to go.

"I've got a wrap." She pointed to a black velvet shawl laying on the chair where he'd sat to view her collection the first time he'd come to her apartment.

"I'll get it," he said, walking over and picking it

up, then bringing it over to her and lifting it onto her shoulders. That was when he spied the tattoo. A dragonfly, about an inch and a half wide, sat at her back right shoulder. He stared at it. A tattoo? He balked inwardly, imagining what his mother would think when she saw it, and she certainly would see it. You couldn't miss it, not in this backless dress.

Damn.

Then he got mad. Why did he care what his mother thought? He was a grown man in charge of his own life.

Yet he couldn't deny that the tattoo, even one as tasteful and attractive as this one, bothered him. He was not the kind of man to enjoy seeing a woman's beautiful skin—and Joanna's skin *was* beautiful— blemished by a black ink drawing, no matter *how* tasteful.

He didn't mention it, though, just draped the velvet over her shoulders and said, "Shall we go?"

He could smell the light fragrance she wore as they rode silently down in the elevator, and he itched to draw her closer. He knew if he placed his lips in the tender curve of her neck, it would be warm there. Just thinking about it, he felt his heart beating a little faster.

He wondered what she was thinking. Did she know how just the sight of her made him feel? Did she have any idea how much he wanted her? How he dreamed about her? How she occupied way too many of his waking thoughts?

Marcus hated the insecurities she'd managed to unearth in him. He despised feeling so out of control, so much a victim of his emotions.

Marcus didn't trust emotions.

Yet since meeting Joanna, he'd been completely in their thrall.

What was he thinking?

Was he glad to be with her or did he wish he hadn't asked her to accompany him tonight?

She wished he'd say something.

He said he liked your dress and that you look beautiful. What more do you want?

She wanted to be tall and coolly blond like his former girlfriend and probably *all* the women he'd dated in the past. She wanted green eyes or violet eyes or a color that was interesting, not the plain brown she was stuck with. She wanted to be sophisticated and confident moving in the circles he moved in.

But as soon as all these thoughts crowded into her mind, she rejected them. What was wrong with her? She didn't really want any of those things. She was perfectly happy with who she was, and if he wasn't, that was his problem.

Had he noticed her tattoo? He must have, when he put the shawl around her shoulders. How could he have missed it?

Yet he hadn't said a word. He probably hated it. He probably thought it looked cheap. Well, too bad if he did. She loved her tattoo. In fact, she was thinking about getting another one, maybe on her ankle.

By now they'd reached the first floor. When they walked outside, she saw that he'd parked illegally in front of her building. And he'd gotten a ticket. She could see it tucked under the windshield wiper.

"I figured it was worth taking a chance," he said.

"I didn't want you to have to walk." He grabbed it and shoved it into the glove compartment.

The ride to the Four Seasons Hotel downtown didn't take long. Marcus offered Joanna his arm as they entered the ballroom, where the benefit was taking place. Sweeping views of Elliott Bay and Puget Sound were the perfect backdrop for the beautifully set tables ringing the dance floor, and the elegantly dressed guests that had already arrived.

Joanna's heart accelerated as Marcus led her to a table where several guests were seated. As they approached, Vanessa, dressed in a short gold beaded sleeveless dress, stood. She gave Joanna a big smile and hug, saying, "I'm so glad Marcus brought you. Here, sit next to me so we can talk."

Joanna glanced at Marcus. "In a minute," he said. "I'd like to introduce you to my mother first."

He led her to the woman sitting two seats away. She looked up. Her grayish-blue eyes, identical to her son's, studied Joanna coolly. "Mother," Marcus said, "I'd like you to meet Joanna Spinelli. She's the designer I told you about, the one who will be showing her work at the gallery in late November. Joanna, my mother, Laurette Barlow."

"It's very nice to meet you," Joanna said. His mother was beautiful. Late sixties, Joanna guessed, mostly from the way she was dressed, because her skin was unlined and her figure youthful and slim. She wore a pale blue satin column gown with a square neckline and long sleeves. A rope of pearls hung around her neck, and small pearl-and-diamond earrings graced her ears. Her hair, silvery-blond, was swept back in a chignon.

"How do you do?" she said. She didn't smile. Her eyes traveled from Joanna's hair to her feet in a slow inspection.

She's a snob, Joanna thought. She straightened and lifted her chin. She remembered what her mother had said the night before. *You're good enough for anyone!*

Sitting between Vanessa and her mother was a distinguished-looking man who also appeared to be in his late sixties, perhaps even early seventies. He had thick white hair, a neat white mustache and bright blue eyes.

"Joanna," Marcus said, "this is Walker Creighton, our lawyer and an old family friend."

Walker Creighton stood and clasped Joanna's hand. "Such a pleasure. You're very beautiful, my dear. But I expect no less from Marcus. He has impeccable taste."

Joanna smiled. What a sweetheart Walker was. She wondered if he was Laurette Barlow's date or simply a guest of the family. "Thank you."

Introductions over, Marcus held out the chair next to Vanessa, and once Joanna was seated, said, "I'll be right back. I need to check in with the chairman."

Joanna turned to Vanessa. "I love your dress."

"My mother picked it out," Vanessa said dismissively. "I really wanted to wear something like the outfit I'm buying from you, but she'd never have let me out the door in pants. I'm lucky I didn't have to wear some prom dress." She said the words *prom dress* as if they left a bad taste in her mouth.

The corners of Joanna's mouth twitched. Vanessa felt like a breath of fresh air in this staid environment. "Most girls would consider themselves extremely lucky to be wearing that dress."

Vanessa looked sheepish. "I know. It is beautiful, and I do like it. I just get so tired of being told what to do and what to wear…and even what to think."

"I know it's hard. I used to chafe at my father's rules. But you'll be on your own soon."

"I can't wait!"

"Exactly what is it you can't wait for?"

Both Joanna and Vanessa startled at the sound of Laurette Barlow's voice, which carried perfectly, even though it wasn't loud.

"The day I can make my own decisions," Vanessa answered without hesitation.

Joanna once again admired Vanessa's lack of fear. Laurette's expression hardened. Instead of answering her daughter, she addressed her next remark to Walker Creighton. "Children can be so thankless, don't you think?"

"They can be, yes," he said, "but I don't think you have to worry about that, my dear. Your children think the world of you and they appreciate everything you've done for them."

Vanessa turned back to Joanna and rolled her eyes. "She makes me crazy," she murmured.

Joanna fought to keep from laughing, because she knew Marcus's mother could see her. "That's a mother's job," she whispered back.

Just then, Marcus reappeared, and soon after, three other guests joined their table: a husband and wife he introduced as old family friends Stephen and Emily Garrett and their teenage son, Jordan, who looked bored and acted as if he wanted to be anywhere but there. Stephen and Emily were friendly, though, and they chatted companionably for a while.

Very soon, the dinner service began, and conversation became more sporadic as they sampled the excellent wines and courses.

"Oh, these scallops are wonderful," Emily Garrett enthused.

"Mine are rather overcooked," Laurette said, frowning.

"We can send them back, Laurette," Walker said.

"I don't want to make a fuss."

Joanna wondered if Marcus's mother was being sarcastic or if she really didn't realize she'd already made a fuss. Joanna's scallops were cooked perfectly. She had a feeling Laurette simply wanted attention.

Emily Garrett turned to Joanna, saying, "I love your dress. Where did you get it?"

"I made it," Joanna said.

"You *made* it!"

"She's a fashion designer," Vanessa piped up. "Her clothes are gorgeous."

"And they'll be shown at Up and Coming the end of November," Marcus interjected. "You'll be getting an invitation, Emily."

"Well, I can't wait," Emily said. She gave Joanna a warm smile. "Do you have a showroom?"

"Not yet, but I'm working on it."

"What about a business card?"

"That I can do." Joanna'd had the foresight to put a couple dozen in her evening bag earlier. She handed one across the table to Emily.

Emily looked at it, then said, "I'll call you."

Joanna was thrilled to have made her first positive contact of the night. And when Marcus reached over and squeezed her leg just above the knee, she knew he was pleased, too. Their eyes met, and in his she saw something that made her heart do one of its silly flips. And just like that, she knew tonight's invitation wasn't about business at all. She'd been kidding herself to think so. Without really thinking, she placed her left hand over his.

"Thank you," she murmured. Then she removed her hand and he removed his, and they both returned their attention to their food. But it took a long time for Joanna's heart to regain its steady, even beat again, and she was acutely aware of Marcus beside her.

When the dessert service began, the chairman of the night's event stood and tapped her wineglass to get everyone's attention. "Welcome to the annual dinner dance benefitting the Hooper Women's Shelter," she said. "I'm delighted to see so many of you here. This year's benefit has broken all records for attendance. And I'm sure the silent auction—which is set up in the adjoining room—will do us proud, as well."

She then went on to introduce her committee and after that, the members of the board of directors, one of whom was Marcus. Joanna couldn't help feeling a swell of pride when he stood to boisterous applause. It was clear from the reaction of the attendees that Marcus was well thought of and well liked.

After the director of the shelter had spoken, the brief program was over and the dancing began. Marcus turned to Joanna. "Let's walk a bit, and I'll introduce you to the people I think you should meet."

Joanna hid her disappointment. She had been hoping he would ask her to dance. But she took his arm and let him lead her around. Soon her head was spinning with names and impressions. He seemed to know everyone, and they all knew him. Most of the women he introduced her to were friendly and asked for her business card, and she felt she was making some good connections. The men were another story. Without exception, they seemed admiring. Several of them made comments to Marcus. One preppy type, someone Marcus obviously knew well, said, "Where have you been keeping *her* hidden?"

Marcus smiled. "I don't give away my secrets."

And just as Joanna thought she'd met everyone and was beginning to hope that maybe now Marcus might suggest dancing, a tall, stunning blonde walked purposefully toward them. Joanna knew immediately who she was. Amanda Warren. Marcus's former girlfriend. And probably his ex-lover. Amanda had a determined look in her eyes as she neared. "Hello, Marcus. I wondered if I'd see you here."

"Hello, Amanda." He leaned over and kissed her cheek.

"Hello," Amanda said to Joanna. "I don't believe we've met."

"Amanda, this is Joanna Spinelli. Joanna, Amanda Warren."

"It's nice to meet you," Joanna said. She thought about extending her right hand, then decided not to.

Amanda studied Joanna for a few moments. "Spinelli. I don't recognize the name."

"I don't normally attend functions like this one," Joanna said.

"Joanna's a fashion designer. A very good one, I might add," Marcus said.

Amanda gave him an amused smile. "Since when have you been interested in fashion?"

"Since I booked Joanna into Up and Coming for a show," he said.

"I see." Her green eyes swept Joanna. "Is your dress one you designed yourself?"

"Yes."

"It's quite nice."

Damned with faint praise, Joanna thought. But she couldn't fault Amanda for it. It must be horrible to see an ex-lover you still cared for—and it was obvious to Joanna that Amanda did still care for Marcus—out with another woman. If Joanna had been in Amanda's shoes, she might have wanted to scratch her eyes out.

"Well, it's been nice seeing you, Amanda, but we were just getting ready to leave."

"I hope you don't mind going," Marcus said after Amanda walked away. "I hate these affairs and never stay any longer than I have to."

They went back to their table, said goodbye to the others—Vanessa hugged Joanna and said she hoped to see her again soon—then exited the ballroom.

They didn't talk on the short drive to Joanna's apartment. This time he didn't park in front. Instead, he drove around back to the garage. Joanna didn't know what to think. Did he want to come up to her apartment? Or was he simply making sure she got safely inside?

They walked around to the entrance and she handed him her key. Inside, she could see Thomas on the phone. He was still talking when she and Marcus entered the lobby, and simply waved at them as they walked back to the elevators.

"I'll see you up," Marcus said.

Should she ask him in? Did she want to?

When they reached her apartment, she opened the door, hesitated for a moment then turned to him. "Would you like to come in?"

He didn't say anything for a long moment. Then, softly, almost gruffly, he said, "If I come in, I want to make love to you."

Joanna's heart went haywire. And it was a few seconds before she could catch her breath enough to answer. "I want that, too. Very much."

And then she opened the door.

Chapter Thirteen

Later, Joanna wouldn't remember them getting undressed. She'd only recall how Marcus had laughed when he'd seen her "bed."

"We're going to have to do something about this," he said in between kissing her. But he gamely fitted himself alongside her on her quilt-covered sofa. After a few minutes of trying to find a comfortable position, he easily lifted her and placed her on top of him. "That's better," he murmured, positioning her between his legs.

Better didn't describe how it felt to lie there, feeling the length of his fit and toned body underneath her, skin to skin, just as if they were two puzzle pieces perfectly matched.

As his kisses and hands became more demanding, Joanna stopped thinking at all. She allowed herself to absorb the sensations pummeling her. She could feel his erection beneath her, hear his ragged breathing, smell the essence of him, and as his tongue tasted and licked, his hands cupped and stroked, she responded with every fiber of her being.

"This isn't going to work," he groaned. "I want to be able to see you."

Laughing, they pulled the quilt off the sofa, doubled it up and lay side by side on the floor. If Joanna thought being on top of him was good, having him able to give every inch of her his full attention was amazing. She knew she shouldn't compare him to Chick, but it was hard not to, for Marcus was a very generous lover and Chick hadn't been. Marcus took his time touching her and kissing her, slowing her down when she would have put her arms around him and urged him to go faster.

"Not yet," he whispered when she reached for him. "Let's enjoy this first."

She cried out when he lowered his head and began to kiss her there, in the place that throbbed and ached. And when he found her sweet spot with his finger, and suckled her nipples at the same time, she thought she might die from the sensations building to a crescendo.

"Oh, oh," she said, arching her back.

His mouth found hers again, and he kissed her deeply as her body shuddered in glorious release. Only then, after she had calmed, did he allow her to tend to him. Joanna hadn't imagined she'd find herself climbing to another peak, but soon enough, she was again at the precipice. And this time, he was right there with her.

But before entering her, he said, "Do I need to use a condom?"

"I'm on the Pill," she managed to say before he thrust inside, pushing deep.

They fit together so perfectly, she thought as those unbelievable sensations assaulted her again. And when she finally exploded, almost in perfect sync with him, she felt like crying. Not because she was unhappy. Because she was so wondrously *happy*. She couldn't remember ever feeling like this before. As if she was finally in the place she was always meant to be. With this man. In this moment. Home. She was at home.

I love him, she thought. *I love him so much.*

That was her last thought before she fell asleep wrapped in his arms.

He'd done it now.

There was no going back. No wondering if he should have or shouldn't have. No second-guessing. He'd taken the leap. For better or worse, he'd made love to this woman, and now he would have to deal with the consequences. And yet he wasn't unhappy. He didn't feel he'd made a mistake. On the contrary, he couldn't remember ever being so content, so satisfied and so looking forward to the future.

Joanna was amazing. He knew he was overusing that word, but he couldn't help it. There was no other way to describe her or the way she made him feel. Simply amazing. Astonishing, even.

He couldn't believe how perfectly she suited him. Even though he was tall and she was little, they seemed made for each other. She'd felt so right in his arms, she might have been designed with him in mind.

He watched her as she slept. He knew he should sleep himself. Either that or get up and go home. But he didn't want to go home, nor did he want to sleep. He'd rather just look at her and marvel that he'd found her. That they'd somehow, against all odds, found each other.

Eat your heart out, Jamison. This woman is mine.

He smiled. Kissed her forehead gently. Whispered that she was wonderful. And then he, too, slept.

* * *

Joanna was dreaming that someone was licking her face. She opened her eyes. No, she wasn't dreaming. Tabitha really was licking her face. Suddenly she was fully awake. Memories of the night before flooded her mind. Marcus! Where was he? She was wrapped in her quilt and on the sofa. The last thing she remembered of the night before was being wrapped in his arms, on the floor.

Had he gone home?

But then she heard the water running. In the shower. He was in the shower. Either that or some intruder was in the shower. Sitting up, absently petting Tabitha, she looked around. No intruder. For there was Marcus's tux tossed over a chair. And there was her beautiful lace gown draped over the TV set in the corner.

Oh, God. She must look a wreck. She'd never removed her makeup last night. Ha. She'd never done *anything* sensible last night.

Oh, but what she *had* done had been wonderful. Remembering, she blushed. She'd been completely wanton.

And she couldn't wait to be wanton again.

Marcus didn't know how anyone could get a proper shower in this ridiculously small enclosure. He could barely turn around. Still, he managed to soap himself and rinse, and the water was satisfyingly hot. He'd also managed to unearth a big, clean towel. Unfortunately he would have to put on yesterday's underwear, and brush his teeth with his finger, but at least he was clean and felt ready to face the day. Drying himself off, he wondered if Joanna was awake yet. He grinned, thinking how adorable she'd looked sleeping. She might not have thought so, but he had enjoyed looking at her, smudged eye makeup and all. In fact, she'd looked good enough to eat this morning. It had taken all his willpower not to wake her and make love to her again. The only thing that had stopped him was the knowledge that he had an appointment with Walker at the Barlow offices at ten o'clock, and he couldn't miss it. They were going to go over his father's will because Tad had gotten a job offer from the software firm where he'd interviewed a week ago and was again making noises about contesting their father's will.

Emerging from the shower, Marcus saw that Joanna was no longer sleeping on the sofa. Then he heard noises in the kitchen. And soon after, he smelled coffee brewing. Following his nose, he entered the small area—more kitchenette than kitchen. She stood at the counter pouring half-and-half into a small milk glass pitcher. She turned and gave him a shy smile.

Adorable was definitely the word, he thought. Amazing, adorable and astonishing. All those *a* words. Her face was clean of makeup, and now he could see the smattering of freckles across her nose. She looked years younger and yes, good enough to eat. Her curvy little body was enclosed in an oversize white terrycloth robe, and her feet were bare. Her toenails were painted black, too, he noticed. He started to laugh.

"What's so funny?" she said.

"You. You like black, don't you?"

Following his gaze, she looked down at her feet. "I do. Is that a problem for you?"

"Let's just say nothing is a problem for me today,"

he said, walking over and pulling her up against him. He bent down and nuzzled her neck. "Um, you smell good."

"It wasn't easy washing up in the kitchen sink," she said. "I heard you in the shower. Did you find everything you needed?"

"I did. Although it would have been nicer having you in there with me." Then he laughed again. "Not that two of us could fit in that thing." Remembering that she was moving, he added, "What's the shower like in the new place?"

"There's plenty of room for two there."

"Is that a promise?" He couldn't resist untying her robe and reaching in to cup her breasts.

"Stop that," she said weakly. But she didn't try to remove his hands. Instead, she leaned back into his embrace.

He sighed deeply and kissed her neck. Then he let her go. "I wish I could stay. But I have a ten o'clock appointment. And it's already nine."

She nodded, and hurriedly tied her robe again. "Do you have time for coffee before you go? I could make some toast, too."

"Do you have an insulated cup? Otherwise, I'll just pull into a Starbucks on the way. I need to get to the office in time to change. I can't meet Walker still dressed in my tux."

"I do." She opened the cupboard over the coffee-maker and took out a tall insulated container. She poured it full of coffee. "Cream? Sugar?"

"No, just black."

She put the cap on the cup and handed it to him. Their eyes met. In hers, he saw a question. Leaning down, he kissed the tip of her nose. "Last night was… amazing."

"It was," she whispered.

"I'll call you later. I have a dinner I have to go to tonight, but maybe we could do something tomorrow?" He wished he could ask her to go with him to Cornelia Fairchild Hunt's dinner tonight, but he knew it would be rude to bring an uninvited guest and it was too late to call Cornelia and ask about bringing Joanna.

"I'm not sure about tomorrow. My best friend is flying in from New York. Look, we'll talk about it later, okay?"

He guessed he'd have to be content with that.

He'd call her later. With some guys, that might have been a kiss-off line. But Joanna knew Marcus wasn't like that. If he had no intention of calling her, he would not have said he would.

Now she wished Georgie wasn't coming, because she knew there was no way she could see Marcus tomorrow. Not on Georgie's first day.

And oh, she did want to see him. She had never wanted anything so much in her life. She still couldn't believe everything that had happened. How he had said if he came in he would want to make love to her. And how she hadn't even thought about it before replying that's what she wanted, too. And then all that fantastic and wonderful sex. But what they'd shared was more than sex, and she knew it. He truly *had* made love to her, and she to him.

You love him. Admit it.

Okay, so she loved him. Was that so bad?

Not bad. But it might be stupid. Only time will tell.

Joanna fixed herself a cup of coffee with a dollop of cream and a packet of sweetener. Yes, time would tell. Maybe she *had* been stupid, but she wasn't sorry.

Walker told Marcus that if he and his mother were both agreeable to allowing Tad to sell some of his stock, there would be no problem with the will. "You know the board will go along with anything the two of you want to do. Within reason, of course."

Marcus had already decided he would buy any stock Tad wanted to sell, so there was no danger of it falling into alien hands. "Thank you, Walker." Marcus started to get up in preparation for leaving.

"Marcus, do you have a few minutes more?" Walker asked. "There's something else I wanted to discuss with you."

"Sure." Marcus sat down again. "I've got some time."

Walker smiled at him. "Your father would be proud of you, you know."

"Thanks, Walker. I appreciate that."

"Your mother wouldn't have been able to manage without you."

Marcus wondered what had brought this on. Walker seldom spoke about personal matters, except where they pertained to finances.

"I'd like to know how you'd feel about your mother marrying again."

Marcus blinked. Of all the things Walker might have said, this was the last thing Marcus had expected. "Why, if she wanted to, and the man in question was someone suitable, I'd be happy for her." Actually he'd be elated. He might even be able to finally have a life of his own.

Walker cleared his throat. He seemed almost embarrassed, but he met Marcus's eyes without looking away. "The man in question is me."

Marcus stared at the man who had been his father's closest friend and confidant. He guessed he shouldn't be that surprised, although he was, mainly because he wouldn't have thought his mother would appeal to a man like Walker, whose deceased wife, Alicia, had been a sweet, homey woman who seemed more comfortable baking cookies with her grandchildren than attending society functions. "I would be honored to have you in our family, Walker. You must know that."

Walker smiled. "I hoped so, but I wanted to be sure."

"Have you and Mother spoken of this?"

"Not in so many words, but I'd like to ask her to marry me, and I think she'll say yes."

She'd be a fool not to, Marcus thought. "Well, if you want my blessing, you have it." He stood then, and held out his hand.

As the two men shook hands, then laughed and clasped each other in a hug, Marcus began to wonder if the earth might be tilting on its axis. First Tad had actually gotten a job, on his own, and then Marcus had thrown caution to the wind and done exactly what he wanted to do concerning Joanna—and to hell with the consequences!—and now it looked as if his mother's future might be assured. Now if only he could get Vanessa squared away, his life might actually approach something resembling normal.

Marcus called at noon. Joanna had decided she was better off suspending work on her designs and instead getting her move under way. Once she was in the new place, with more room to work, she could concentrate on finishing everything she needed to finish for her show. First things first.

So she was making a list of everything she needed to do, in the order she needed to do it, when her cell rang. Seeing Marcus's name, she felt her heart lifting and she was smiling when she said hello.

"Hi," he said. "What're you doing?"

"Making a list of everything I need to do to get ready for my move."

"I see."

"You sound disappointed."

"I did hope you were thinking of me."

She laughed softly. "I've had a hard time thinking about anything else today."

"Good. Because I can't stop thinking about you, either."

Just hearing his voice made her breath quicken.

"Since you're busy tomorrow, I was hoping I could come by and take you to lunch."

Joanna thought about the million and one things she should be doing today. Needed to be doing today. "Okay. When are you coming?"

"I can be there in thirty minutes."

"I'll be ready. I'll wait downstairs."

Thirty minutes later, when he pulled up to the curb, she practically flew outside. She didn't even care that Thomas, watching from inside her building, could see the way they kissed before Marcus helped her into the car. And how they kissed again once he got in beside her.

"Where are we going?" she said breathlessly as he pulled out into traffic.

"I brought a picnic lunch." He inclined his head toward the backseat where she saw a wicker basket covered with a cloth.

"You packed a lunch?" she said in disbelief.

He smiled wryly. "I can't take credit for it. Franny, our cook, did it for me."

Joanna imagined he was taking her out by the water somewhere, so she was puzzled when fifteen minutes later he pulled into the garage of a high-rise condominium building.

He explained that they would have their "picnic" in the corporate suite his company kept for VIPs.

"So I'm a VIP?" she teased.

"You certainly are. A *very* important person." By now they were in the elevator that would whisk them to the eighteenth floor. And while it was whisking, he was again kissing her.

The picnic didn't get eaten until two hours later, because in the meantime, Marcus decided she had to see the king-size bed in the main bedroom, and then he suggested they might like to try it out. "Knowing what you sleep in, I think we're going to be spending a lot of time here," he said.

Making love with Marcus in a big comfortable bed was even better than it had been the first two times in her apartment. Afterward, they lay together, spoon fashion, while one hand lazily caressed her breast and the other stroked her belly with occasional forays even lower. Joanna sighed in contentment and wished she could stay like this always.

She hated to see the afternoon end, but at four o'clock Marcus said he needed to take her home because he was due at the Hunt mansion at seven and needed time to get ready. "I wish I could take you with me tonight."

Joanna was glad he couldn't. She wouldn't have known how to act in front of Cornelia and Harry Hunt. She wanted to keep her new relationship with Marcus a secret for a while. Maybe she wouldn't even tell Georgie what had happened.

For the rest of the day she hugged the knowledge to her that Marcus had wanted to be with her, not just today, but tonight and tomorrow, too. Maybe she'd worried about their differences for nothing. Maybe he really didn't think she needed to change to fit into his life.

And yet she still felt a tiny niggle of doubt. It was too soon to be certain of anything. This might last, or it might not. But no matter what happened, even if eventually Marcus tired of her and decided to move on, even if the present was all she had, she would extract every drop of pleasure and joy out of it. She would seize the day and emulate her favorite heroine, Scarlett O'Hara, and not worry about tomorrow.

Although Marcus would have loved to have Joanna with him, he enjoyed the evening with the Hunts. The only other guests present were Harry's son, Alex, and his wife, P.J. Marcus took to both of them immediately. They were charming, friendly and fun. The conversation was lively and the food exceptional. Cornelia and Harry were wonderful hosts who made you feel at ease almost immediately.

After they were served their dessert—a delicious apple tart—and coffee, Cornelia turned to Marcus.

"I was so pleased to hear you decided to give Joanna Spinelli a show."

Marcus smiled. "Yes, she's very talented. I think the show will be a big success."

P.J. seemed interested, so Marcus and Cornelia explained. "She's Georgie's best friend," Cornelia added at the end.

"Really?" P.J. said. "Do you know her, Alex?"

Alex and Georgie, although not related by blood, had been close friends from the time they were kids, explained Cornelia.

"We both met her, at Georgie's wedding," Alex said.

"I had forgotten," P.J. said. "That was such a hectic day with all the little kids there and all."

"Georgie thinks the world of her. Actually, I think Joanna's pretty special myself," Cornelia said. She smiled at Marcus.

Did Cornelia suspect something? Marcus wondered. Was she looking at him in a strange way? Well, what did it matter if she did suspect his relationship with Joanna was more than that of a business partner? Did he really care?

That night, as he drove home, he decided he didn't care *who* knew about him and Joanna. In fact, people knowing would be a good way to test the waters and see if she could comfortably fit into his life on more than a temporary basis.

And in the meantime, he would make the most of being with her every chance he got.

Chapter Fourteen

Joanna ended up telling Georgie about Marcus. She couldn't help it. She was so happy, yet confused, and she had to talk to someone. Besides, Georgie would have guessed anyway. She and Joanna were spending most of every day together. So while they were packing and organizing, Joanna used Georgie as a sounding board.

"Do you think I'm making a mistake?" Joanna asked.

"Do *you*?" Georgie countered.

"Honestly? I don't know." She smiled ruefully. "I hope not."

Georgie nodded. "I hope not, either. I don't want you to get hurt."

"I know. I don't, either. But I'm a big girl. I went into this with my eyes wide-open, and if I get hurt, I get hurt."

"I'm not sure your eyes *were* wide-open," Georgie said thoughtfully.

"Of course they were. Are. I know exactly why we're wrong for each other."

"You say that, but I'm not sure you believe it. I think you're just like the rest of us. You've convinced yourself that love is magic. That Marcus will somehow turn into the kind of man you want him to be. We all think we'll change the things we don't like. But the truth is, most people don't change. They are who they are."

They are who they are. Joanna kept thinking about Georgie's words. She was terribly afraid Georgie was right. After all, hadn't Joanna said the exact same thing more than once? *I am who I am.* She wanted Marcus to accept her as she was and not try to change her. So why did she think he should change?

All too soon, it was time for Georgie to return to New York. Once she was gone, Joanna and Marcus fell into a routine. Every evening, when she was finished for the day, she would text him. And unless he had a commitment he couldn't break, he would drive over and either pick her up and take her to dinner somewhere or bring takeout and they would eat at her apartment. If they had dinner out, they'd go to the corporate suite afterward and spend a couple of hours making love. If the corporate suite was host to a visiting VIP, they'd stay at Joanna's. He always left by three, though. Even though Joanna said she didn't care what anyone thought, she didn't want Thomas gossiping about her, and she knew him well enough to know he would.

Joanna couldn't wait to move, so the weekend after Georgie went home, Joanna moved into her new quarters. Her brothers and father all helped, and Marcus provided a van from his company, as well as two men to assist with the heavy lifting, so the move was accomplished in less than four hours.

Joanna had ordered a kitchen table and chairs as well as a queen-size bed for the new apartment, and the delivery took place the afternoon of the move, so along with her mother's and sister-in-law Sharon's help, the kitchen, bedroom and bath stuff were unpacked and put away and the apartment was ready to inhabit before six. Joanna picked up Tabitha from the vet's, where she had been boarded. The two of them would christen the new place by spending the night.

Marcus was attending a meeting of the board of directors of one of his many charities, and Joanna was actually glad to be alone. She was tired, for one thing, and for another, she'd hardly had time to think lately. It was kind of nice to be alone and quiet, with no one to consider but herself.

She ate pizza for dinner, took a shower and was settled into her new bed by ten. At ten-fifteen her cell rang. She smiled when she saw it was Marcus.

"How'd everything go?" he asked.

"Great. They were finished moving me in by two."

"I'm sorry I couldn't help out today."

"Don't be silly. You were a huge help, sending that truck and the two men. We had plenty of help. My dad and all my brothers were here."

"I would have liked to meet them."

Joanna bit her lip. She would have liked for him to meet them, too, even though part of her was afraid of how such a meeting might go. Marcus was so different from the men in her family. She couldn't picture them talking, considering that her brothers' conversations mostly consisted of whether or not the Seahawks would have a winning season, the Mariners might be in line for the pennant this year or what crappy thing their bosses had pulled that week. And politics! Forget about it. If her brothers got started on politics, no telling what would happen. She cringed just thinking about it.

"I thought I might come by tomorrow," he said.

"I need to finish unpacking and get my workroom set up."

"I can help."

Joanna knew what would happen if he was there. Yes, he would help, but sooner or later—probably sooner—he would distract her by kissing her or touching her, and then they'd get no more work done. "Wait and come about six, okay?"

"You drive a hard bargain, woman. Okay, six it is."

Before Joanna knew it, October was over. She felt as if all she'd done was blink and the month had disappeared. Looking back, she believed that despite her doubts about her relationship with Marcus and where it would ultimately end, October was probably the happiest, most perfect month she'd ever had. Georgie, true to her word, had helped her find two assistants—both talented and proficient needlewomen and good workers—so her days were spent happily designing clothes and learning to work with Nim and Tanya. And most of her nights were spent with Marcus.

She blushed even thinking about how much time they spent in bed. And if not in bed, in the shower together. Or taking a bath together. Or cuddling on the sofa. And sometimes they even necked in the car because they couldn't wait until they were inside her apartment.

During that entire month, there was only one incident that upset Joanna and intensified all her buried doubts. She and Marcus had just had some really sensational sex and, sated, were lying in bed lazily talking. She lay on her stomach and Marcus lay on his side.

He was stroking her back and once in a while he'd lean over and kiss her. At one point, he traced the dragon-fly tattoo on her right shoulder and casually said, "Is it painful to get a tattoo removed?"

She had been about to say, "I don't know," when she realized what he'd asked and what must have prompted the question. Abruptly, she sat and drew the quilt up to cover herself. She stared at him. "You don't like my tattoo, do you?"

He met her gaze squarely. "It's not that I don't like it…"

"Don't lie to me, Marcus. You hate it, and you want me to get rid of it. That's why you asked the question."

He shrugged. "I don't hate it. It's true that I don't like seeing skin as beautiful as yours spoiled by a tattoo and that I'd prefer you didn't have it, but I don't hate it."

"I love my tattoo, and I'm not getting rid of it. So if that's what you think, you can just put it out of your mind."

"You won't even discuss the possibility?"

"Why should I? I see nothing wrong with it." She glared at him. She was so mad she had half a mind to go out and get another tattoo. And this time she'd get it where everyone could see it. All the time!

He didn't say anything, but his silence was more eloquent than any words would be.

"What else is wrong with me that you'd like to change?" she demanded.

Now he sat up, too. "Maybe we should drop the sub-ject until you're in a more reasonable frame of mind. In fact, it's late, and I have a meeting early tomorrow, so I'd better get going."

"I'm perfectly reasonable," she said through gritted teeth. "You're the one who's not. Do I keep find-ing fault with you?"

He sighed wearily. "Joanna, you're exaggerating. I do not keep finding fault with you."

"Really? Do you think I'm stupid? Do you think I don't know why you compliment me so much when I wear what you consider 'suitable' clothes? Do you think I don't realize how much you hate my makeup and hair and nail color? Just because you don't say it in so many words doesn't mean I don't know what you're thinking."

"I didn't know you were a mind reader," he said evenly. But his eyes had turned colder than the top of Mount Rainier. "And I also don't know why you're trying to pick a fight with me. It's not going to work. I'm tired and I have to be up early tomorrow. I think it's best I leave. Give us time to calm down before we talk again."

Joanna knew he meant *she* needed to calm down, but dammit, she didn't want to. She wanted to have this out once and for all. He didn't approve of her, and he wouldn't admit it. Instead, he just made not-so-subtle remarks. But even as angry as she now was, and as much as she wanted to get everything out in the open, part of her knew it wasn't a good idea to force a confrontation. They weren't kids playing truth or dare. They were two adults involved in a more-serious-every-day relationship, and if she had any hope at all of salvaging it, she'd better cool down. So even though it killed her, she said, "That's probably a good idea."

Women could be impossible sometimes.

Marcus drove home too fast, because the more he

thought about Joanna's totally uncalled-for and unreasonable reaction to a perfectly innocent question, the more indignant he got.

But because he really was a fair and honest man, by the time he was in his own quarters and readying for bed, he admitted to himself that his question about the removal of tattoos hadn't been as innocent as he'd pretended.

She was right. He didn't like the tattoo. He didn't *hate* it, but he did hate the fact that she had one. He knew he was being a snob, but there was something about a tattoo that felt cheap to him. And he knew the people in his circle probably felt the same way. Perhaps that, more than anything, bothered him. He might say he didn't care what others thought, but down deep, he did. *Doesn't everyone?* he wondered. *Doesn't Joanna?*

Maybe he needed to get an answer to that last question. Because if Joanna truly didn't care what others thought, maybe there was no hope for them after all.

"I'm sorry about last night."

Marcus nodded, even though Joanna couldn't see him since they were talking on the phone. She had called him, waiting until early afternoon. "I'm sorry, too," he said.

"We can talk tonight, if you like, and I promise not to get upset."

He smiled. "I'll be there by six."

She kept her promise. She didn't get upset, not even when he admitted he wished she didn't have the tattoo.

"Well, I do have it. And yes, it's terribly painful to have them removed. Besides, I don't want to. If…if you don't want to keep seeing me because of it, just say so."

He couldn't help admiring how much courage she had. Even though they disagreed, he was proud of her for standing up for herself. He remembered how the first time he met her, he'd seen her as a worthy opponent. She was that, all right, and more. Suddenly he was ashamed of himself for making such a big deal out of a small tattoo.

"Come here," he said, his voice gruff with emotion. After that, they didn't talk.

The following day Joanna had just finished cutting out a pattern for a dress she intended to make out of white eyelet when Marcus called.

"I meant to tell you about this last night," he said, "but I got distracted." He chuckled.

"Tell me about what?"

"My mother and Walker are having a small engagement party here at the house Saturday night, and I'd like you to come."

Two things popped into Joanna's mind: the disapproving look in Marcus's mother's eyes the night of the benefit and the fact that she, Joanna, had nothing to wear. "I... Okay. Um, it's not going to be formal, is it?"

"No. I'd say a cocktail dress would be perfect."

Joanna sighed. She didn't own a cocktail dress. She wasn't a cocktail party type of person. She wondered if she could get away with black velvet pants and her silver sweater.

"What's the matter?" Marcus said.

"Nothing's the matter."

"It's not like you to be so quiet. Don't you want to go?"

"Yes, of course, I want to go." *Liar.* She didn't want

to go at all. In fact, if she never had to see the snobby Laurette Barlow again, it would be too soon. It had been very clear to Joanna what Laurette thought of her, even if Marcus didn't seem to realize it. "It's just that I don't have time to make a dress, and I honestly have nothing to wear."

"That's easily fixed. I'll buy you a dress."

Joanna began to protest, but Marcus wouldn't listen. "It's settled. We're going shopping. You can take a couple of hours off tomorrow afternoon, can't you? I'll pick you up at two o'clock. We'll go to Nordstrom."

Joanna knew it was useless to argue. Marcus was determined to buy her a new dress, and truth to tell, she was curious to see what he would deem suitable.

She actually liked the dress he wanted to buy. It was a Kate Spade organza and beautifully made and detailed. But she wanted the dress in black, which they had, and he kept insisting she would look better in the pink. "I'm not a pink kind of girl," she said.

"It looks wonderful on you," the saleswoman said. She obviously knew who would be writing the check.

Joanna looked at herself in the three-way mirror. The pink was so *pink*. She'd so much rather have the black. If the saleswoman hadn't been standing there listening to every word, Joanna would have told Marcus he must have forgotten that argument they'd had because he was at it again—trying to change her to fit his vision of the ideal woman.

And then Marcus did something so sweet and so thoughtful that Joanna could feel all her arguments melting away. He turned to the saleswoman and said, "Would you mind giving us a private moment?"

"Oh, of course not, Mr. Barlow. Just press this buzzer when you want me."

Once she was out of earshot, he said, "Look, Joanna, I'm sorry. If you want the black, I'll buy the black for you. But I wish you'd wear the pink instead. It looks fantastic on you."

After that, what could she say?

He bought her the pink.

Typical of November weather, Saturday-night temperatures fell into the low forties. Joanna dug out her black wool coat and wished she had something nicer-looking to wear.

Marcus sent a car for her, and she had to admit it was very pleasant to ride in luxury and not have to worry about traffic or anything else. When the driver pulled into the circular drive in front of a beautiful stone mansion—there was no other word for it—she could only stare. Wow. The place was lit up like a Christmas tree, even to the tiny white fairy lights in the shrubs surrounding it. She had always known she and Marcus came from two different worlds—how could she not?—but the contrast between her parents' little three-bedroom and finished-attic bungalow and this behemoth was stark…and inescapable.

Marcus stepped outside as soon as the car stopped. And he opened the door for her, and helped her out. He even kissed her hello in front of the driver. The kiss made Joanna's butterflies settle a bit, but not for long, because the moment she walked into the beautifully decorated house, she felt all her insecurities come flooding back.

Ohmigod. The house was *Architectural Digest* fodder. Gorgeous hardwood floors, Oriental carpets, a magnificent chandelier, a winding staircase like ones you see in the movies, flowers and candles everywhere and the soft buzz of conversation coming from the direction of what Joanna imagined to be the formal living room. "The house is beautiful, Marcus."

He nodded. "I can't take any credit for it. My father had it built for my mother when they married. He was a good bit older than she was, and I think he felt as if he'd won a prize or something."

"Well, it's lovely."

A maid took Joanna's coat, and Marcus, putting a proprietary hand on her waist, led her into the living room, where a dozen or so people were gathered. He headed straight to his mother, who stood near the fireplace with Walker Creighton at her side. Laurette looked perfect, as Joanna imagined she always did, in a dark blue velvet dress and the same pearls she'd worn to the benefit dinner. She was smiling and talking to another older couple as they approached.

Marcus waited for a lull in the conversation, then said, "Mother, Joanna's here."

The bright smile faded, and Joanna could see the older woman had to make an effort to keep her expression pleasant. "Hello, Joanna. So glad you could come."

"Hello, Mrs. Barlow, Mr. Creighton. Thank you for having me. And congratulations on your engagement."

"Thank you, my dear," Walker Creighton said. "I'm a lucky man." So saying, he put his arm around Laurette and smiled down at her.

Marcus introduced her to the other couple, a Dr. and Mrs. Arnold, then led her away to introduce her to the other guests. The next few minutes were a swirl of names and impressions, which Joanna was afraid she wouldn't remember. And then Marcus steered her toward Vanessa, who stood by the piano talking to an extremely good-looking young man. Her spirits lifted. Marcus's mother might not approve of her, but she knew Vanessa didn't feel that way.

Vanessa was once again wearing the short gold beaded dress, which Joanna had discovered was a Vera Wang design. No wonder it was so beautiful.

"Joanna," Vanessa said, giving her a hug. "I'm so glad to see you again."

"And this is our brother, Tad," Marcus said, indicating the young man, who Joanna now saw had the same bright blue eyes of his sister. His hair wasn't as dark as Marcus's or as light as Vanessa's, but more a medium-brown with gold highlights. Just the way he stood, his careless smile and hooded gaze as he gave her a once-over, told Joanna everything she needed to know. He was a bad boy. And he liked being a bad boy.

"Well, well, Marcus," he said, "where have you been keeping *her* hidden?"

"Behave yourself, Tad," Marcus said.

Tad directed his next remark to Joanna. "My brother is the staid, conservative one in our family. The women he normally dates never look the way you do." He smiled. "You're more *my* kind of woman."

"Don't pay any attention to him," Vanessa said. "He likes to shock people." Turning to him again, she said, "Joanna is an extremely talented fashion designer. She and I are going to be showing our designs at Marcus's gallery later this month."

"I'll have to be sure to come," Tad said.

"Would you like something to drink, Joanna?" Marcus said. He ignored his brother.

"I'd love a glass of wine."

He squeezed her waist. "I'll be right back."

"Don't hurry," Tad said. "I'll keep her occupied." Moving to her side, he put his arm around her.

Joanna didn't want to be rude, because after all, Tad *was* Marcus's brother, but she didn't like him. Deciding his bad manners didn't deserve a reward, she pointedly removed his arm and distanced herself.

"What's wrong?" Tad said. "Worried about what old Marcus will think? He's a cold fish. Haven't you noticed?"

"Oh, for God's sake, Tad," Vanessa said. "Grow up! Or if that's impossible, go find yourself another juvie to play with."

Just in time to hear the last of what his sister had said, Marcus returned with two glasses of wine and handed Joanna one. "Tad never learned how to act in company," he said.

Joanna wondered what her parents would think about the Barlows and their relationships. If she hadn't thought so before, she definitely knew it now—she had a wonderful family. They might not have the Barlows' money and social position, but they had something infinitely more valuable. They loved and respected one another.

No wonder Marcus was so uptight.

She felt sorry for him.

The last of her insecurities disappeared. She had no reason at all to feel inferior to him or to his family. And she certainly didn't need to change to be accepted by them.

If Marcus wanted her, he would have to take her as is.

Chapter Fifteen

Joanna's family always made a big deal out of Thanksgiving. Ann Marie said it was her favorite holiday because no one had to buy gifts or feel obligated to do anything but enjoy the day. Joanna loved the holiday herself. Turkey and her mom's old-fashioned bread dressing were her favorite food in all the world. She didn't even mind the way the men all collapsed in the living room after dinner to watch football while leaving the women to do all the cleanup.

When she discovered that Marcus and Vanessa would be alone for Thanksgiving, she was appalled. "But where will your mother and brother be?"

"My mother and Walker are going to France. She wants to introduce him to her family, most of whom still live in the Burgundy Valley. And Tad is going to New York to stay with his college roommate."

"But that's terrible! You can't be alone."

"It'll be fine, Joanna. It's not like it's the first holiday we've been on our own."

But Joanna couldn't imagine anything worse than Marcus and his sister rattling around that huge house alone. "You're coming with me to my parents' house for Thanksgiving. Both you and Vanessa."

"I don't think—"

"I won't take no for an answer," she said, interrupting. "We eat about three, but everyone comes early so we can visit. It's very casual dress. My brothers will all be in jeans."

Marcus said he and Vanessa would swing by and pick Joanna up at one o'clock.

Thanksgiving day dawned cold and rainy. Joanna spent the morning working on a color-blocked shift dress that was the last piece of her youth collection. Then she took a quick shower and dressed warmly in her black boots, black jeans and a black-and-white cable-knit sweater. Her contribution to dinner, a green-apple pie, was already in its carrier. Making sure Tabitha had fresh water and enough food to last her all day, Joanna made her way downstairs and waited for Marcus just inside the door. He pulled up outside a few minutes later.

Vanessa had been sitting in front but got out to give Joanna that seat and climbed in the back. Soon they were on their way.

"It's so nice of you to have us today," Vanessa said. "I'm looking forward to meeting your family."

Joanna noticed Marcus didn't echo his sister's sentiments. She wondered what he was thinking. Was he as uneasy about meeting her family as she'd been about his? Well, it had to happen sooner or later, especially if they were to continue their relationship, and he'd given no indication otherwise. At the very least, today promised to be interesting.

Two other cars were in the driveway when they arrived, but there was room for Marcus's, and Joanna told him to park there. She wondered what her brothers and father would think when they saw the Ferrari.

Wonderful smells and boisterous laughter greeted them when they walked in the front door, followed by warm smiles from Joanna's parents, who had walked into the entryway. "I'm so glad to finally meet you!" Ann Marie declared.

"Thank you for having us," Marcus said. "This is my sister, Vanessa."

"Such a beauty," Ann Marie said. "Joanna told me you're going to model one of her designs on Saturday."

Vanessa smiled. "Yes, I'm really looking forward to that."

"Oh, we are, too. We can't wait for the show," Ann Marie said. "Can we, Tony?"

Joanna's father looked at Marcus. "Don't mind her. She's wound up. She always talks too much when she gets wound up." He shook Marcus's hand and winked at Vanessa.

"Oh, Tony," Ann Marie said.

"Come on, Marcus, Vanessa. Let me introduce you to my brothers," Joanna said. Leading him into the living room, she saw that Tony and Sharon weren't there yet, nor were Michael and his wife, Leslie. Joey and his fiancée, Beth, sat on the sofa, and Billy stood nearby. Joanna made the introductions and was amused to see that Billy, normally voluble, seemed dumbstruck as he stared at Vanessa.

She did look gorgeous today, Joanna thought, in her figure-hugging jeans, high brown boots and a blue sweater the exact shade of her eyes. Her wonderful hair fell in shining waves and she looked healthy and young and sexy all at the same time.

Joey, at least, managed to talk to Marcus semi-intelligently, although quickly enough, the conversation turned to football. Joanna rolled her eyes. "Billy, why don't you get drinks for Vanessa and Marcus? I'm going out to the kitchen to see if Mom needs any help." Marcus was a big boy. He didn't need her there to run interference.

Beth followed her to the kitchen. "Thanks for rescuing me," she said. "I'm so sick of football."

Joanna laughed. "Join the club."

Ann Marie said she didn't need help yet, that everything was under control. "Your father helped me earlier."

"Really? Is the sky falling?" Joanna said.

"Now, Joanna, be fair. Your father helps out a lot."

"In what universe?" Joanna looked at Beth. "Hope you know what you're getting into in this family, Beth."

Beth smiled. "I'm Irish, remember? My family is just as bad, if not worse."

"I like your Marcus," Ann Marie said. She had just finished putting the last deviled egg on a serving dish and handed it to Joanna. "Here. You can put this on the coffee table."

"He's not my Marcus," Joanna said. She took the plate.

"I haven't known you to bring a man to Thanksgiving dinner before," her mother retaliated.

"I felt sorry for them. They were going to be alone."

"Have it your way. But I do like him."

I like him, too. Joanna walked into the living room, where she saw that Tony and Sharon were now being introduced, followed by Michael and a very pregnant Leslie, who was due to give the Spinellis their first grandchild on Christmas Eve.

Marcus's gaze met hers. His expression gave nothing away, and maybe that troubled her more than anything else. She guessed this was the way he looked when he was negotiating a deal. It was a poker face, the kind of mask you adopt when you don't want anyone to know what you're thinking.

Joanna hugged Leslie and Sharon, greeted her brothers, and then turned to Marcus. "Are they taking care of you in here?"

"Of course we are!" Joey said. "He's tried the sausage balls and the shrimp, and I fixed him a drink. What more could he want?"

"Good." Joanna smiled at Marcus. He returned the smile, but it seemed forced. He was uncomfortable, and couldn't entirely hide it. She looked around. "Where's Vanessa?"

"Billy wanted to show her his bike," Joey said.

Oh, no. Joanna could just imagine what Marcus had thought of that. Billy's bike was his baby. He'd bought the Honda NC700X used last June and loved to show it off.

"They were taking off for a ride when we drove up," Mike said.

"But it's raining," Joanna said. She couldn't even look at Marcus, afraid of what she'd see. Damn Billy. She'd like to choke him.

"The rain stopped," Sharon said. She gave Joanna a sympathetic look.

But the streets would be slippery. And Joanna knew without being told that Marcus didn't approve. She just hoped Billy didn't try to show off, that he drove safely, that he'd made Vanessa wear a helmet and that they came back soon. And the moment she could get him in a private corner, she'd give him a piece of her mind.

"I warned him to be careful," Joanna's father said.

Joanna moved to Marcus's side. "You doing okay?" she said softly.

"I'm fine."

He was so far from fine. She knew he was upset, and honestly, she didn't blame him. It had been totally clueless of Billy to take Vanessa out on the bike. Couldn't he have seen that Marcus didn't want her to go?

It seemed like hours before Billy and Vanessa returned, but it was only about twenty minutes. They walked in laughing, bringing good spirits and cold air with them.

"Oh, that was so fun!" Vanessa said. "You'd *love* it, Marcus, the way you love speed."

"Yeah, that car of yours is cool," Billy said. He grinned at Vanessa. "Does he let you drive it?"

"Are you kidding? He won't even let me breathe on it."

Throughout this exchange, Marcus remained stone-faced. If looks could kill, Joanna thought, her heart sinking. It had been a mistake to invite Marcus and Vanessa today. Why couldn't she have waited? They would have met her family at the show on Saturday, and that would have been an easier first time for all of them. She glanced at her watch. It was only two o'clock. Why was the day dragging so much?

Finally it was time for dinner. The dining room table could comfortably seat eight, but somehow Ann Marie had managed to squeeze twelve chairs in. Normally Joanna loved lots of people around, but today was not a normal day.

Throughout dinner, as her noisy family did all their noisy, Spinelli-like things, Joanna could see the way

Marcus was judging them and finding them wanting. When Billy, by mistake, took the spoon out of the bowl of mashed potatoes and licked it, then said, "Oops," and put it back in the serving bowl, she wanted to crawl under the table. Everyone else laughed, and her mother said, "A few germs won't kill us," but Joanna saw the look on Marcus's face. *Oh, God.* And it didn't help that Vanessa, who Billy had made sure was sitting next to him, laughed along with everyone else.

When dinner was over, she knew Marcus could hardly wait to leave. But he'd been brought up to be polite, no matter what, and polite he was. He listened to her father, he discussed the college football scores, he declined another drink saying he was the designated driver and he managed to keep from glancing at his watch too often. But at six o'clock, he stood. "I need to be going. I'm sorry, Joanna, but I've got a full day tomorrow."

She nodded. "It's fine. I do, too." She could hardly believe it was only two days until the show. But even if it hadn't been, she was just as anxious to get out of there as he was. The day had been a disaster.

But it wasn't over yet. Because Vanessa then said, "Billy's going to take me home, Marcus. So you can stay as long as you like at Joanna's."

Joanna knew Marcus wanted to say something, but what could he say? It wasn't as if Vanessa was a kid. She was going to be twenty-one in January, old enough to make her own decisions, as she'd pointed out to him more than once.

"We're thinking of catching the late movie at the Landmark," Billy said, "so she'll be home late."

The only thing Marcus said was "You're not going on that bike, are you?"

"Nah," Billy said, "we're taking my truck."

As they walked out the door—Joanna with leftovers her mother insisted she take—Joanna didn't have to wonder anymore what Marcus was thinking. She knew. And what he was thinking didn't bode well for their future.

Marcus wanted nothing more than to be alone. Yet here was Joanna, sitting beside him, and he knew he had to at least make an attempt to act as if nothing was wrong.

Could the day have been any worse?

Could her *family* have been any worse?

Sure, her parents were nice people, and they'd tried to make him feel welcome, and her brothers were okay. Well, all except Billy, who was obviously spoiled rotten and had no manners to speak of. He also didn't have good sense. Marcus had wanted to kill Vanessa for the way she'd acted around Billy. Bad enough he couldn't keep his eyes off her, but she'd actually encouraged him. Billy Spinelli was not the kind of man Marcus wanted for Vanessa. Marcus wasn't even sure what Billy did for a living. When he'd asked, Billy had blithely said he'd just started a new job and wasn't sure if he liked it yet. "I'll let you know when I figure it out," he'd added, laughing as if it was a big joke.

Christ, the kid reminded Marcus of Tad, although Marcus didn't think Billy had a drug problem. Damn. He guessed he'd have to put his foot down with Vanessa, let her know in no uncertain terms that this thing with Billy could not continue.

Why had he let Joanna talk him into going to her family's house today? He'd known it wasn't a good idea, but he'd gone anyway.

"Marcus, are you going to give me the silent treatment all the way home?"

Marcus started. He'd almost forgotten Joanna was in the car with him. "Sorry. I'm tired and I'm afraid I ate too much."

"Then maybe you should just drop me off. I'm tired, too, and as you pointed out, we both have big days tomorrow."

Marcus knew he should contradict her, but he couldn't face more hours of trying to pretend everything was fine when it wasn't. He needed to be alone. He needed to think.

So when they arrived at her place, he got out and made sure she was safely inside, gave her a quick kiss good-night and said he'd call her in the morning.

As he drove home, he faced an inescapable truth. All along he'd been thinking in terms of changing Joanna to fit into his world, but today he'd finally realized how much he would have to change, too, if he wanted her as part of his life. Could he? He found her family intimidating with their boisterous behavior and the way they advertised their emotions so openly. He wasn't sure he could ever be comfortable around them.

He knew he wasn't going to come up with a magical answer. Not tonight, anyway. He only hoped that by tomorrow his head would be clearer. Because he could not go on like this.

Joanna felt sick at heart. Today had shown her so clearly that she would never be able to live up to Marcus's standards. Eventually he would realize this, too—if he hadn't already—and then he would dump her. But even as she told herself this, there was still a tiny spark of hope that she was wrong.

She decided to test him. So when he called her at ten the next morning, she said she thought they needed to talk. He agreed and said he'd stop by at five. She sent Nim and Tanya home at four so she and Marcus could have privacy. All the work for the day was finished, anyway. And both women would be coming in early tomorrow to help her transport everything to the gallery for the show, which would begin at five.

When Marcus arrived, Joanna was ready. Nervous, but ready.

"I've been thinking," she said when they were settled upstairs in her living room, him on the sofa, her in her favorite rocking chair opposite him.

His gaze met hers. "I have, too."

Taking a deep breath, she said, "I think, once the show is over, we need to take a break from each other."

His gaze never wavered. The moment stretched. It was so quiet in the room she could hear Tabitha eating in the kitchen. He nodded, almost imperceptibly. "I agree."

Joanna's heart sank. If he'd said no, he didn't agree with her, she would have known he loved her no matter what, and that he was willing to try, perhaps even to change. But he didn't say no. Which meant that he, too, believed they'd never make it together.

He left soon after, but not before gathering her into his arms and kissing her softly. It was all she could do not to cling to him, not to say she hadn't meant it.

"I'll see you tomorrow," he said, releasing her.

"Yes."

At least the tears didn't come until after he'd walked out the door. And then they came like a cloudburst. She cried all evening and far into the night. Why had she ever allowed herself to fall in love with him? It was utterly hopeless and always had been. Down deep, she'd known that, but she'd gone and done it anyway. She was a stupid fool. Despite all the odds against her, she had gambled, and she had lost.

She deserved to be miserable.

The show was on its way to becoming a huge success. Everyone who was anyone in Seattle society was there: Cornelia and Harry Hunt, tons of people who said they worked with Marcus on this committee or that committee, all of Joanna's family and friends. Georgie and Zach had flown in from New York, all of Georgie's sisters and their husbands were there, too, and even Alex Hunt had come, per Georgie's invitation.

Several members of the press had shown up, too, including Shea Weatherby, a writer Joanna admired enormously. Shea turned out to be really nice, and she interviewed Joanna at length. "You're going to be a big star," she predicted. "I wish I could afford to buy that color-blocked shift. It's just gorgeous." Joanna felt like hugging her. Maybe she should give her the dress.

Joanna's collection, Vanessa's jewelry and Jamison's paintings were all big hits, and both Brenda and Peter, her assistant for the evening, were kept busy taking orders. Joanna couldn't have been prouder, but none of the triumphs of the evening could make up for the fact that underneath her smile, Joanna was miserable.

This would be the last night she would ever see

Marcus. That certainty throbbed inside. She could see he knew it, too, because he stayed away from her the entire evening. And she saw how he watched Vanessa and the way Billy was hanging all over her. She wished Billy would cool it. But then she thought, why should he cool it? If he liked Vanessa, there was no reason not to let her know it. He was just as good as she was. And Joanna was just as good as Marcus, and if he was too blind to see it, he didn't deserve her.

She was better off without him.

Although Marcus kept his distance, he couldn't stop looking at Joanna. His misery over the past twenty-four hours had shown him something: he didn't want to live without her. Since she'd entered his life, he hadn't once felt lonely. He loved her; he'd finally admitted it to himself, and he wanted her. But more important, he had been wrong all along. She didn't need to change. *He* did. But could he? That was the question of the night. Could he?

While his thoughts were still going in this vein, Jamison walked up to him to thank him. "I'll never be able to repay you for what you've done for me, Marcus."

Marcus stirred himself enough to smile and say, "No repayment is necessary. I believe in your work. I'm happy to have the opportunity to show it."

"This is such a great night!" Jamison said. He couldn't seem to stop smiling.

"Yes, it's even more successful than I imagined it would be."

"And it's all due to you."

"I just gave you the venue to show your work. You and Vanessa and Joanna are the real stars."

"Joanna! To think I might not have met her!" His face glowed as he watched her talking to a nearby group. "Isn't she beautiful? Now that this show is behind us, I can make her my number-one priority."

After Jamison drifted off to talk to a potential buyer, Marcus wondered if he should have said something about his relationship with Joanna. Was it fair to let the younger man think the field was clear? And yet what could Marcus have said? For all he knew, Joanna wanted nothing more to do with him and would welcome the attentions of Jamison. That thought made him feel sick. What could he do to ensure that Joanna would realize how sincere he was about changing? And to let her know how much he loved her? Suddenly an idea niggled at the back of his mind.

He was turning it over, wondering if it would be enough, when Cornelia approached to remind him she and Harry were hosting a reception for Joanna at their home after the show was over. "You'll be there, won't you?"

He forced himself to smile warmly. "If I can, I'll drop by later on. I have something important I need to do."

"Oh. Okay."

Marcus could see she was bewildered. Of course she would expect him to be there. He took her hand and squeezed it. "I really will try."

As she walked away, Marcus realized he had disappointed her. He seemed to be doing a lot of that lately. Maybe he needed to change even more than he'd imagined.

* * *

Cornelia couldn't imagine what could be so important that Marcus would skip Joanna's celebration. Had they had some kind of disagreement? Now that she thought of it, she hadn't seen them together at all tonight. Spying her husband standing alone by the bar, she joined him and slipped her arm through his.

"I just don't understand it," she said after telling Harry about her conversation with Marcus. "I thought he was in love with Joanna. I thought he'd probably *bring* her to the party." She sighed. "I wonder what's wrong. Maybe there's something I could do…."

"Now, Cornelia," Harry said, patting her hand, "it's not a good idea to meddle in the love lives of others."

"As if you ever followed that advice," she scoffed. She was very disappointed. Marcus and Joanna made such a wonderful couple. Why couldn't they see it?

Later, she even mentioned this to Frankie, her second oldest daughter, who teased her a bit, saying, "Now, Mom, aren't you satisfied that the show is such a success? I didn't think matchmaking was part of the deal when you decided to be Joanna's fairy godmother."

"It's not," Cornelia said pensively. "But still… they do make such a lovely couple. I am glad my efforts to help Joanna's career have paid off so handsomely, though." She smiled. "It's fun playing fairy godmother."

"Maybe you should go into business," Frankie said, laughing. "You know, become a professional fairy godmother."

"I know you're joking, but the truth is, I *have* been thinking along those lines," Cornelia said. "I mean, I might as well put that money Harry gave me to good use."

"Seriously? You want to be a professional fairy godmother?"

"Why not? There have to be a lot of other young women out there who need a helping hand. As a matter of fact, I've already talked to Harry about opening an office and hiring someone to work for me so I can continue mentoring young women who are trying to establish businesses." She gave Frankie an exasperated look. "And in typical Harry fashion, he's already bought me a building in Ballard! I wanted to kill him when he first told me, I mean, he thinks he can run everything, but I've gotten over it. Actually I'm glad I don't have to do the legwork of looking for a place. Instead, I can concentrate on looking for a helper."

Frankie stared at her. "Mom, you continually amaze me."

"What? You don't think this is a good idea?"

"I think it's an amazing idea. And you know what? I know just the person who might be persuaded to help you get your fairy godmother business started. Her name is Felicity Granger, but everyone calls her Phil. She's got the perfect background. Tomorrow I'll give you her phone number, and if you're interested, you can call her."

Cornelia smiled happily, temporarily forgetting about her disappointment over Joanna and Marcus. "It's a deal."

Joanna wasn't surprised when her mother told her she'd overheard Marcus telling Cornelia he wouldn't be at the reception Cornelia was hosting. She was surprised, though, when Billy told her Vanessa was going with him. Joanna would have thought Marcus would put the brakes on that.

The show was over at nine, but it was nearly ten by the time the group arrived at the Hunt mansion. Everything looked so beautiful, Joanna thought. There were fresh flowers everywhere and a combo played soft music for dancing and the dining room table groaned with a fabulous array of food. Champagne flowed freely, and two bartenders served the guests anything else they wanted to drink.

And sitting in the place of honor on the mahogany buffet was an enormous cake decorated in pink. *Congratulations, Joanna!* was written across the top.

Some of Joanna's pleasure and excitement in the evening faded as midnight came and went and Marcus still hadn't shown up. People kept remarking on the fact that he wasn't there and asking her where he was. It was horrible. She had to keep a smile on her face and pretend everything was fine, that he just had other commitments. The only person who understood was Georgie.

"I'm so sorry, Jo," she said at one point.

"I know. Me, too."

"Maybe there's some kind of family emergency he had to tend to."

"You really think so? And that's why Vanessa is here having such a good time?" Joanna glanced over to where Vanessa and Billy were doing an energetic cha-cha.

"Did something happen between you two?" Georgie asked gently.

Joanna wanted to pour out her heart to Georgie, but

she knew if she did, she would break down and cry. And she couldn't break down. Not here. Not yet. "I'll tell you tomorrow, okay?"

"Okay." Georgie leaned over and kissed her cheek. "Chin up."

Joanna nodded. At twelve-thirty, as some of the older guests were beginning to make noises about leaving, she finally had to face it. Marcus wasn't coming. He, like she, had realized their worlds simply couldn't mesh. She would most likely never see him again, unless for some reason their paths crossed at the gallery where her work would stay on display for the next week.

At one o'clock, Joanna—who was fighting off a headache—headed toward Cornelia. "Cornelia, thank you for everything," she said. "I can't tell you how much I appreciate the lovely party."

"It was my pleasure, Joanna."

Joanna smiled and hugged the older woman. She had just started to say that she was going to call it a night when there was a stir among the crowd. Turning to see what had caused it, Joanna felt her heart nearly stop.

Marcus had come.

He stood just inside the arched entry to the ballroom. He was looking at her. And everyone else was looking at him.

Joanna couldn't breathe. She was afraid she was going to faint. Why had he come? She wasn't sure she could handle anything else tonight, especially if he was going to ignore her the way he'd done at the gallery.

But he didn't ignore her. Instead, he headed straight toward her and when he reached her, he pulled her into his arms. And then, in a voice everyone could hear—especially since the moment he'd put his arms around her the entire room fell silent—he said, "Joanna, I love you.

"I love you just the way you are. I don't want you to change even one hair on your head, and I want to spend the rest of my life with you."

He released her long enough to reach into his jacket pocket and pull out a small black velvet box. Snapping it open, he removed a gorgeous antique diamond ring. "This belonged to my French grandmother," he said, "And I want it to be yours. You've changed my life, and I don't want to live without you. Will you marry me, Joanna?"

Joanna trembled. She was afraid to trust what he'd said. She wanted to, but she was so scared.

And then he did something she knew she would remember for the rest of her life. He removed his jacket and rolled up the left sleeve of his shirt. "This is why I didn't come earlier," he said.

She stared at his left biceps. Maybe he was serious. Maybe he really did love her enough to stop trying to change her. Because Marcus had gotten a tattoo! Two beautifully rendered initials—a *J* and an *M* entwined together inside a heart now adorned his biceps. "That's where I was all this time," he said, grinning. "Do you like it?"

"I love it!" Laughing, she wrapped her arms around him. "Of course I'll marry you."

When they kissed, the onlookers all clapped. And every woman in the room had a lump in her throat and tears in her eyes. Everyone loved a happy ending.

Epilogue

From the pages of Around Puget Sound *magazine:*
Marcus Barlow Finally Takes a Wife
by Phoebe Lancaster

This past Saturday evening, just one month after giving her his French grandmother's antique engagement ring, Marcus Osborne Barlow III wed Joanna Marie Spinelli at St. Dominic's Catholic Church in Georgetown. As most of you who read my column regularly know, Marcus has been the most eligible bachelor in this area for a long, long time, and area women have despaired of his ever succumbing to Cupid's bow. But the fair Joanna, the up-and-coming fashion designer who recently had a sensationally successful show at the real Up and Coming, stole his heart and snatched him from under the noses of all those other hopeful women.

Acting as best man was longtime Barlow family friend and lawyer Walker Creighton. Georgie Fairchild Prince was Joanna's matron of honor. The bride wore a simple white satin gown of her own design and carried a cascading bouquet of stephanotis and ivy. Her grandmother's lace mantilla adorned her head.

The newlyweds are building a home on the Barlow Estate and, after a honeymoon in Italy—where the bride has always wanted to go—they will begin their new life as Mr. and Mrs. Marcus Barlow.

PS: The bride confessed to me privately that she and her new husband are expecting a little Barlow in approximately seven months. Oops!

* * * * *

REQUEST YOUR FREE BOOKS!
2 FREE NOVELS PLUS 2 FREE GIFTS!

*Damien Bravo-Calabretti was the
Playboy Prince of Montedoro, until innocent Lucy Cordell
asked Dami to be her first. Will this bad-boy prince fall for
the sweet beauty under the mistletoe?*

***

She shook that finger at him again. "Dami, I may be inexperienced, but I saw the look on your face. I felt your arms around me. I felt…everything. I know that you liked kissing me. You liked it and that made you realize that you *could* make love with me, after all. That you could do it and even enjoy it. And that wasn't what you meant to do, when you told me we could have the weekend together. That ruined your plan—the plan I have been totally up on right from the first—your plan to show me a nice time and send me back to America as ignorant of lovemaking as I was when I got here."

"Luce…"

"Just answer the question, please."

"I have absolutely no idea what the question was."

"Did you like kissing me?"

Now he was the one gulping like some green boy. "Didn't *you* already answer that for me?"

"I did, yeah. But I would also like to have you answer it for yourself."

He wanted to get up and walk out of the room. But more than that, he wanted what she kept insisting *she* wanted. He wanted to take off her floppy sweater, her skinny jeans and her pink tennis shoes. He wanted to see her naked body. And take her in his arms. And carry her to his bed and show her all the pleasures she was so hungry to discover.

"Dami. Did you like kissing me?"

"Damn you," he said, low.

And then she said nothing. That shocked the hell out of him. Lucy. Not saying a word. Not waving her hands around. Simply sitting there with her big sweater drooping off one silky shoulder, daring him with her eyes to open his mouth and tell her the truth.

He never could resist a dare. "Yes, Luce. I did. I liked kissing you. I liked it very much."

***

We hope you enjoyed this sneak peek from
USA TODAY *bestselling author Christine Rimmer's new Harlequin Special Edition book,* HOLIDAY ROYALE, *the next installment in her popular miniseries*
The Bravo Royales, *on sale December 2013, wherever Harlequin books are sold!*

HSEEXP1113